# Granada
# Gold

## S A CARNEY

Matador
9 Priory Business Park
Kibworth Beauchamp
Leicestershire LE8 0RX, UK
Tel: (+44) 116 279 2299
Fax: (+44) 116 279 2277
Email: books@troubador.co.uk
Web: www.troubador.co.uk/matador

ISBN 978 1783060 276

British Library Cataloguing in Publication Data.
A catalogue record for this book is available from the British Library.

Typeset in Aldine401 BT Roman by Troubador Publishing Ltd
Printed and bound in the UK by TJ International, Padstow, Cornwall

**Matador** is an imprint of Troubador Publishing Ltd

*For Roger*

Kingdoms of Spain 1492

# PART I
# Riding South

F rightened to let him go, I circle my arms tighter around his neck.

"I love you, *querida*." He uses the Spanish word for dearest. Today is my twelfth birthday, and he leans down to kiss me goodbye. "I'll come back. I promise. I never break my promises, do I?"

I press my cheek against my father's, rich with the scent of horses and leather, wild lavender and polished steel. He pries my hands away and rises.

My brother stands close beside me and our father hugs us. "Take care of your mother." He leaves unsaid, *if I am killed at Granada*.

Our mother is part-English and is devoted to prophesies. I tremble, for they say we live in the end of days, and omens surround my family this year in 1491.

My father rides to the siege of Granada; there is only one man I trust to save his life. He watches us across the crowded plaza of Fort Santa Fe: the English warlord Edmund Sales. His bay stallion pounds its front hooves repeatedly, throwing clouds of dust. The army must move out.

Lord Sales pushes his horse through the soldiers to get near us; a close friend of King Henry Tudor, he commands the volunteer company of English longbow archers in the Granada War. He tugs his sword from its scabbard, the blade mirror-bright in the Andalucian sun.

"Long live King Fernando!" Lord Sales shouts in his own English language, saluting my father. Then he pivots in his saddle to face the Christian army and yells *"Viva! Viva el rey Fernando!"* The soldiers, Spanish and English alike, roar in approval *"Viva!"* hammering weapons and shields. *"Viva el rey Fernando!"*

King Fernando of Aragon: my father, and their commander who must lead them to victory.

✠

Lord Sales has fought at my father's side for four years. When his ship first arrived from England, I waited at the river port of Seville with my mother and my brother, to watch the English archers disembark. Lord Edmund Sales could not speak Spanish, but we had a young Irish priest who was our interpreter.

Our priest taught me a simple English greeting, but I was shy about speaking English and my words were muddled.

Don Edmundo – as we called him – knelt down on one knee in front of me, to hear me better. I looked back at my mother and she nodded permission; I greeted him as I would a Spanish relative, kissing him gently on both cheeks. I was puzzled to see his eyes fill with tears. Only later would I discover why.

Our priest said that Lord Sales had fought for Henry Tudor, and helped him win the throne of England. Then Edmund Sales told the newly-crowned English king that his only wish was to enjoy the peace, at his home in Kent, with his wife and young family. It was time to plant orchards of apple and cherry trees, and watch his children grow.

Initially, life was good. Then the killing epidemic of sweating sickness ravaged southern England. It was an enemy against which Lord Sales' sword was powerless. Between one sunset and the next, his wife and his three boys and young daughter died. He prayed to God to take him, too. He thought, with those he loved gone, his own life was over. What did it matter if he accepted King Henry Tudor's request to fight for the Christians in Spain? He had never been to Spain. God only knows what awaited him. He gathered a volunteer troop of longbow archers in Kent and sailed from Dover.

Waiting for him when he landed in the port of Seville was the Queen of Castile and two of her children. A little girl named Juana, so like the young daughter he had lost, a girl who spoke shyly to him in muddled English, and had kissed him in welcome.

✠

In the plaza of Fort Santa Fe, my father raises his hand in acknowledgement to Lord Sales and the army. His handsome face is freshly barbered; his hair is darker than mine, with silver wings at his temples. He is clean-shaven, like all our Christian soldiers, with his hair cut short. Our Moorish enemies are bearded, with long hair coiled under their turbans. In combat, my father has just one glance, one instant, to know friend from foe.

He reaches into his doublet to retrieve his good-luck talisman, which he always carries. "A birthday gift for you, *querida*." He touches it to his lips, and hands it to me. "It will bring me more luck with you to keep it safe."

The talisman feels warm and fits snugly into my palm. It is a carved cameo portrait in a gold frame edged with rubies that glisten like drops of blood. The face is that of a queen.

"She was the most beautiful woman in the world," Papa says, placing his fingertips under my chin. "You look just like her. Always remember that, Juana."

My father's words make my heart sing. The portrait is of his grandmother, Merina de Cordoba. *The legendary Merina de Cordoba, the Jewish beauty who captured the heart of a Christian king and became the matriarch of a great dynasty. In my wildest imaginings, I can't see how I – Juana the shy, the wayward – can ever grow up to be like her.*

I clasp the jewel tightly, my legacy.

A man-at-arms brings my father's war horse forward and he swings into the saddle. He advances the grey stallion, neck arched and prancing against the bit, to the front of the church, where my mother waits for him.

*"Viva la reina Isabel!"* Papa bows his head in tribute to her. My mother pauses, her gloved hand on his horse's mane. She reaches up on tiptoe as my father leans down from the saddle to kiss her farewell.

"Long live Queen Isabel!" Lord Sales shouts, his eyes devouring my mother. I know that Lord Sales and the officers love my mother; the soldiers of her own Kingdom of Castile worship the ground she walks upon.

*"Viva los reyes!* Long live the Christian monarchs!" the soldiers cheer, and my brother and I shout ourselves hoarse. I raise my fist holding the jewelled portrait above my head. I pray to God: *I swear I will keep my father's talisman safe for him, and You, dear God, please bring my father and Lord Sales home to*

*me. If it is to be the end of the world as some people say – or a terrible new age with turn of the century – we will go together, our Trastamara family united.*

My mother ascends the church steps and waits by the great closed double door. My father reins his war horse back.

Santa Fe's bells peal, louder and with great urgency, and in response the doors slowly open. From the cool interior darkness, the great icon known as the Silver Cross is carried into the burning sunlight of the plaza. The cross is the height of two men and its beams are thick as tree trunks; it is mounted on a plinth, borne by twelve sturdy bearers all marching in unison.

The crowd falls silent; the officers on horseback, Lord Sales and the king, my father, all sheath their swords and bow their heads. The Silver Cross is preceded and followed by priests in red-and-gold embroidered vestments, swinging incense burners, sending coils of indigo smoke spiraling into the sky.

Blessed by the cross's shadow, my father and Lord Sales and the cavalry knights gallop from the plaza of Fort Santa Fe, to secure the way for others to follow. I hold my breath until Papa disappears from my sight. I lean against my brother for comfort.

The bells cease and the drums begin, the loud marching drums, hammering their pulsing cadence. The solemn procession of priests and bearers advance, step-pause, step-pause, and the cross sways slightly on its plinth as it is carried forward. It will lead the army to the front line of battle.

The Silver Cross is followed by marching columns of Spanish infantry soldiers, with their pikes and crossbows and arquebuses. They are the hardened veterans of the twelve-year Granada War, the war that began the year that I was born.

After the Spanish infantry come the English company of archers, 300 strong, with their unique longbows slung across their backs, each bow as long as a man is tall. The English archers are the most exotic foreigners I have ever met; they smile and salute as they stride past me, for they have adopted me as their mascot.

At the end is the artillery train, 140 great cannons to break the walls of the last Moorish stronghold, the invincible fortress-city of Granada. The heavy cannons are drawn by spans of oxen, their horns swinging slowly to the rhythm of each ponderous hoof striking the dry earth.

✠

"Papa will win the battle and come back to us." My brother's words comfort me. He is only a year older than me at thirteen, and when we were babies Papa nicknamed us *'los gemelos,'* the twins, because we look so alike and share the same saint's day of San Juan. My brother and I take after our father's side of the family: olive skin with oval faces, wide-set dark eyes with thick black lashes, and slim athletic bodies.

Our mother has blonde hair and beautiful English eyes of blue-green. She named my brother and me for Saint John the Evangelist, *San Juan Evangelista*, writer of the Book of Revelation. My brother, Juan, and me, Juana.

She says that Juan and I might look alike, but our temperaments are opposites. Juan is bright and outgoing as the sun; I am his shadow, wanting only to be near him, the moon reflecting his light.

Our mother fervently believes that Juan is specially blessed, with a divine destiny. I once overheard her praying, "God willing, one day my son Don Juan will become the Spanish king who will fulfill the Granada Prophecy and lead us to the New Jerusalem. Some say the prophecy is about my husband, King Fernando, but I know that the prophecy is about our son." My mother refuses to believe that the end of days is imminent; she is confident that her God will guide her victorious Christian army to conquer the Moorish Kingdom of Granada, claim its vast treasure, and crown her only son as its king. Our land of Spain holds three communities in an ever-shifting uneasy balance of power: we Christians, the Islamic Moors, and the Sephardic Jews.

With the army gone and the plaza nearly empty, Juan pulls his handkerchief from his sleeve and gently pats the dusty tear-streaks from under my eyes. "Give me the portrait, just for a minute." He holds it next to my face. "You really do look just like our great-grandmother."

Our mother stands like a statue on the church steps, her chaplain, Father Cisneros, at her elbow. She frowns when she sees Juan comparing me to the portrait of Merina de Cordoba. Father Cisneros exchanges anxious sidelong glances with the Castilian courtiers surrounding her.

I see that same pained look on my mother's face each time my father praises – as he frequently does – my striking resemblance to Merina de Cordoba, his Jewish grandmother. My mother tells her lady-in-waiting that she has nothing against the Jews. Her trusted treasurer Don Isaac Abravenel is

Jewish, as is our royal family's personal doctor. "But why does my husband keep reminding everyone of that *converso* in his family? There's too much danger in that, these days."

*Converso.* I know what that word means. It is what we call someone who was Jewish, but converts to the Christian faith, as Doña Merina de Cordoba did. '*Converso*' once signified acceptance into Spanish society, but now the Inquisition is determined to test loyalty of every *converso*, and the descendants of all *conversos*.

My parents are distant cousins from two branches of the Trastamara family. The Castilians of my mother's side pride themselves on their solid Christian forebears, and their part-English heritage. The Catalans of my father's Kingdom of Aragon value practical politics over ethnic pedigree. Catalan royal men are susceptible to beautiful women, no matter what their religion.

Juan gives the portrait back to me. "I think Mama wants us."

I tuck the jewel into my bodice.

Mama removes her gloves and lifts the circlet of gold – the Crown of Castile – from her hair. My mother's strawberry blonde hair, without a trace of grey, is gathered at the nape of her neck into an intricate knot, so heavy that it seems her head is always tilted back from its weight. She hands her gloves and her crown to her lady-in-waiting and dismisses her courtiers. Father Cisneros remains at her side.

Queen Isabel is petite, and even at the age of forty her skin is flawless. She looks like her English grandmother, Catherine of Lancaster, and my mother is very proud of her English ancestry.

Queen Isabel speaks little of her grandmother's language. Until the arrival of Lord Edmund Sales and his English archers, we children couldn't speak English at all. Now my brother and I are learning to converse with Don Edmundo, as we call Lord Sales. In return, we are teaching him Spanish.

We kiss Mama dutifully, Juan first, then me. "Growing up, the two of you." She smiles at Father Cisneros. "Soon I must make suitable marriages for all my children. Especially Juan." She softly ruffles her son's hair, and her hand remains caressingly on his shoulder.

Father Cisneros beams. "Perhaps your son could contract a marriage with King Henry Tudor's little daughter. The English alliance is very important."

"Ah, but little Margaret Tudor is just a tiny baby. That means years and years before a proper wedding. I would like to live to see my grandchildren grow up, Father."

Juan winks and gives my hair ribbon a tug. "If we need an English alliance now, maybe Juana should marry Don Edmundo."

"Don't be impertinent," my mother says sharply. "Lord Sales is even older than your father. Consider him an honorary uncle."

"I don't ever want to get married. I just want Papa to come back."

My mother nods in agreement, and briskly takes control. "Today we look to Granada. Juan, my angel, can you help me get the supplies ready? We must load the mule trains and send them to your father's headquarters, before the rains come."

Our soldiers get their supplies carried by endless columns

of thousands of pack mules; it is the only way to get weapons and food through the mountains to the Christian army camp near Granada. It is early November; when the long rains begin, the new road – built by the army – will become impassible.

"Can I help too, Mama?" I ask eagerly.

"No, *querida*. You should join your sisters. Isabella is with the doctors and the nursing nuns, getting the hospital ready for injured soldiers. Would you like to help her?"

I shake my head.

"Then you should join your younger sisters. They're sewing a new altar cloth for Father Cisneros to use when, God willing, we are in Granada."

I roll my eyes. "Today is my birthday."

"Yes, it is, and who should know that better than your own mother?"

This morning, November 6th, 1491, when she came into the bedroom I share with my three sisters to wake us, my mother kissed me first and wished me blessings for the coming year. Mama never says so, but I think she worries more about me than she does about my sisters. *"Juana is like steel that has been too highly tempered. The edge is keen, but the blade snaps under strain," my old nurse told her.*

My eyes darken to dull black at my mother's refusal to let me join Juan.

"Your father says you look like Merina de Cordoba, little one, but your stubbornness is English."

"I want to stay with Juan. We can take our falcons hunting and kill partridges to send to Papa at the front."

"Juana, you cannot always do whatever you want,

12

whenever you want. Your father and the soldiers need bread and meat now, not the luxury of partridges."

I scuff the toe of my boot into the ground.

"Don't worry, Juana," my brother whispers. "We'll go hunting tomorrow."

Father Cisneros clears his throat for attention. He bows to my mother. "Excuse me, Doña Isabel. I must meet the Habsburg ambassador."

"I regret I can't receive the ambassador myself. Reassure him that this is no slight on his master. Tell him I hold the Habsburg Emperor in my greatest esteem, but my army is my first concern. I will talk to the ambassador after we take Granada."

"I'll go get my sewing kit," I say dispiritedly. I turn and drag my boots through the dusty street toward our family quarters.

The room I share with my sisters is simple, lined with wooden sleeping plinths and bright woven wool carpets, with plump cushions stacked and blankets neatly folded. All four of us sisters – Isabella, Juana, Maria, and Catalina – have our individual mule chests in which to keep our personal clothes, books and treasures.

I rummage to the bottom of my mule chest to retrieve my sewing bag. Then I fold my best brocade shawl on top of everything inside, and carefully arrange the portrait of Merina de Cordoba against the turquoise folds. I run one fingertip over the carved cameo and pray with all my heart for my father to be safe. I close the lid. The talisman should be safe here; no one comes into this room but us and our most trusted servants.

✠

I walk, slowly and reluctantly, to the building next to the church, to join my sisters.

The building is traditional Andalucian, with rooms leading off the central open patio. My two younger sisters are seated on cushions near the well in the center of the patio, in the shade of a reed awning. I join them. Usually we laugh and talk, squabbling noisily over threads and colours and designs. But today, we can think only of our father and the soldiers marching to Granada.

Father Cisneros enters the patio; with him is a stranger whom I have never seen before, a man of about thirty years old, walking heavily, as if his feet hurt. He wears a priest's gown of black wool – of a foreign weave and weight – frayed at the hem and travel-stained. My sisters and I scramble to our feet to curtsey.

Father Cisneros introduces us to Father Adrian Boyens, the ambassador of Maximilian Habsburg, the Holy Roman Emperor. He explains that Father Adrian has arrived from the emperor's homeland of Austria.

I stand back and wrinkle my nose when Father Adrian gets close, for he is sweating profusely and he smells like a goat to me. Why don't foreigners from the North bathe?

Father Cisneros speaks in Latin, not Spanish, to the stranger. "You can see that Lady Juana takes after her father. Lady Maria and Lady Catalina look like their mother, Queen Isabel."

Father Adrian runs a thick finger across his lower lip; the

nail is broken. My sisters stare at him with wide blue eyes. I back away, suspicious. *Obviously, this northerner can't understand Spanish, because they are talking in church Latin. I wonder if he walked all the way from Austria to Andalucia?*

Father Adrian turns to Father Cisneros and says, "These two blonde little girls could pass as royal princesses of Austria, or Flanders, or indeed any northern kingdom of Christendom. The dark one looks Jewish to me."

I understand Latin – in spite of the man's heavy northern accent – and I glare at him in outrage. I am furious and hurt by his remark about 'the dark one.' *Why, I take after my great-grandmother – the most beautiful woman in the world – my father says so.* I fire back, "My father asked your emperor to send him soldiers, but the only thing he sends is you, fat priest."

Father Cisneros intercedes hurriedly. "Lady Juana knows Latin, she studies it with her brother. She can also be quick-tempered." He takes his guest by the elbow and leads him to a bench on the far side of the patio. The two priests seat themselves uneasily side by side.

My sisters and I return to our sewing, but my hearing is keen. I viciously stab the needle into the cloth with every stroke, hushing my sisters, and listen to what the priests are saying about us. Father Cisneros, independently of our mother, is matchmaking.

"Lady Isabella, the eldest sister, is working at the hospital today. Lady Isabella is twenty years old, her mother's namesake, and takes after her in looks."

"I've heard that Isabella is engaged to the King of Portugal?"

"Engagements can be broken," Father Cisneros says

eagerly. "I know your master, the Habsburg emperor, has been a widower for many years. Lady Isabella is the most suitable in age."

Father Adrian shrugs. "The Emperor likes young girls. Are these promised yet?" He gestures toward me and my sisters.

"No, not yet. The pretty blonde is young Lady Maria. You see her trying to bring Lady Juana out of her sulks. Lady Maria is always bright and happy. Not very good with her lessons, but a charming, cheerful child. She's eight years old."

Father Adrian nods. "And the youngest?"

"Ah, little Lady Catalina. Look how seriously she takes her sewing. And she's only six years old. Her mother's favourite daughter. A truly Christian child, with all the virtues of a saint."

"That dark girl – Juana – she's the one closest to her brother, I believe?"

"Lady Juana and Don Juan are inseparable. Their father calls them 'the twins', for they are only a year apart in age and the resemblance is so strong. Don Juan is loved by everyone. He is an extraordinary boy, and the only son."

"Before the king and queen had their son, who was the heir?"

"Why, the eldest sister, Lady Isabella, was the heiress – with the title 'Princess of the Asturias' – until the birth of Don Juan. For seven years, she was Queen Isabel and King Fernando's only child."

"Seven years is a very long time between babies. Did Queen Isabel suffer miscarriages?"

"No, but the queen did not conceive for many years. Then

Don Isaac Abravenel, the royal treasurer, brought a new doctor to court, a cousin of his."

"A Jew?"

"Of course. Most of our doctors are Jewish."

"And I suppose his Jewish potions worked their magic?"

Father Cisneros looks offended. "Don Juan was born, to everyone's great joy, thanks to prayers of the king and queen, and the divine intercession of the blessed Virgin Mary and Saint John the Evangelist. But – even so – our Jewish doctors are highly skilled."

Father Adrian sighs heavily. "I've travelled across half of Christendom to meet the Queen of Castile. Now you tell me that she doesn't have time for me. At least you were able to show me the girls." He stands up from the bench and brushes the folds of his gown. "We can go now. I need to pack for my journey and report to the emperor."

"I'm sorry I could not get you an audience with Queen Isabel. She refuses to see any ambassadors or petitioners until Granada is taken."

"Come now, Father Cisneros, I'm not deaf and blind. I know Queen Isabel and King Fernando always find time for the English. I'm very disappointed."

"Please, don't be offended. There will be time for everyone once Granada is taken."

"Perhaps. *If* you win Granada." Father Adrian says. "It's known throughout Christendom that if King Fernando and Queen Isabel lose this battle, they will be completely ruined."

"Ruined? I hardly think that. They keep their faith, and they love their children. Their family is their greatest treasure, above all the gold in Spain."

"If Fernando is defeated at Granada, there won't be any Trastamara family left. The father dead on the battlefield; the mother and her precious son prisoners of the Moors; these girls probably auctioned off to the sultan of Morocco."

"We have faith that God will grant us victory," Father Cisneros says stubbornly.

"Keep praying for that miracle, Father Cisneros. I'm going back to Austria." Father Adrian pauses, and stares across the patio directly at me. "But first, I will go to Seville."

A look of alarm crosses Father Cisneros' face. Everyone knows that Seville is the headquarters of the Inquisition, the *converso* hunters. He follows the foreign priest out of the courtyard.

I look up from my sewing, and shiver as their shadows pass, feeling as if a cold wind blows across my grave.

✠

That night, I find it hard to sleep, for I have nightmares about my father in battle. It is a terrible dream, for I am there with him – not at Granada, but on a great warship, in a storm at sea. I have never sailed the ocean in my life, we are a land-based people, but in my dream the sea feels familiar. Enemy troops have boarded the ship, and my father is fighting for his life. My brother is fighting the enemy, too. Tides of blood run under my feet on the deck. Through the storm the men keep fighting, shouting, the clash of steel on steel. Great waves wash the wounded overboard, howling. I fear for my father and my brother. I am standing close to the mast, watching my brother fighting across the ship, and then he falls over the ship's side, stopping his descent into the ocean by grabbing the rail with his hands. He is holding on. I run to help Juan, but a priest in black robes pushes past me, carrying a large wooden cross, and I think he is going to my brother's rescue. Then he raises the cross and, in fury, smashes my brother's hands, until the bones stick whitely through the skin and Juan releases his grip and plummets into the sea. The priest turns toward me, and I see the face of Father Adrian Boyens.

I wake in a sweat of tumbled bedclothes, my heart racing. I try to calm myself, listen to the breathing of my sisters and my mother in the room. When my father is away, my mother moves into the bedroom I share with my sisters.

Oh my God, my brother! I panic, thinking something has happened to Juan. My brother's bedroom is next to ours, and my terror subsides when I hear the sounds of quiet music. I know my brother is awake, for I hear the plaintive melody he plays on his guitar.

*Perhaps the dream means something terrible is happening to my father at the front line at Granada.* I creep in the dark to my mule chest, where I take out my father's talisman. *"It will bring me even more luck with you to keep it safe."* I take the cameo of Merina de Cordoba back to bed with me, nestling it under my pillow.

*If the talisman is safe, my father is safe.* We are bound to this extraordinary ancestor, Merina de Cordoba. Perhaps this dream is a warning from her. I wonder what she would make of that vile Father Adrian Boyens. If she were alive today, would Father Adrian try to drag her off to the Inquisition? *I pray Father Adrian Boyens hurries back to his Habsburg Emperor in Austria, and I never have to see him again. Ever.*

I fall into a fitful sleep at last, and my mother doesn't wake me for early Mass. The sunlight streams through the shutters, and I touch the portrait under my pillow. I quickly say my morning prayers, shaking off the residue of the nightmare. It was a bad dream, and I resolve to dismiss it. My old nurse once said that we must only reveal bad dreams to God and our confessor, for telling others gives evil more power over us. And who can keep secrets better than a child?

I take the jewel back to my mule chest. I hesitate, debating whether I should keep Papa's talisman with me, or leave it here? I kiss the portrait before I put it inside the chest.

I select clothes for riding. I want to do something special for my father today: Juan and I will take our falcons hunting, and get partridges for him! My father's favorite meal is a casserole of partridges, the birds simmered for hours with pepper and herbs in a huge red pottery dish on the coals of the campfire. The tender meat, falling off the delicate bones, is picked out of a steaming rich broth of olive oil and garlic and saffron. At meals shared together, our family sits on cushions in a circle, eating from the communal dish with our fingers, the air rippling with lively talk and laughter. My gift of partridges will remind my father of happy family times together.

I walk through Santa Fe's strangely empty streets; during the summer, the war-fighting months, the fort was packed with armed men readying themselves for raids outside the fort, raids to burn the rich farms of the Moors, uproot their almond trees and olive trees, destroy their mills and break their irrigation channels, denying the City of Granada food supplies and water.

"We will roll up the Moors' Kingdom of Granada like a

carpet," my father explained in his war plan to Lord Sales. "We will start at the edges of their territory and finish with their capital City of Granada."

Now our army closes the net. Soon, I pray. *Let this final battle end soon. Let Papa and Don Edmundo be safe in the fighting.*

I try to push the worries away, and find my mother and brother. My mother raises her eyebrows when she sees my riding clothes – the divided skirt, the boots, the lightweight short linen cape over my blouse. My hair is combed back into a long braid, tied with a red ribbon. I hold my hat, flat-crowned and broad-brimmed, the hat I wear when riding out in the Spanish sun.

My mother looks from me to Juan.

"Could we go hunting today, Mama, please?" Juan asks. "Just for a few hours?" It is rare for our mother to refuse Juan anything.

"No, my angel, not today. I still need your help with the mule trains, Juan, and your sister needs to finish her sewing."

Tears sting my eyes as I watch my mother and brother walk away from me toward the mule corrals. I clench my fists and jam my hat on my head. I never analyse situations, never seek compromises the way Juan does; I only react to my feelings. I want to go hunting, not sit around sewing with my little sisters. *If Juan abandons me, I will go hunting alone.* I set my jaw firmly, and march to the south of the camp where our family horses are stabled, avoiding the mule corrals.

Our royal Trastamara family, and the army officers of Fort Santa Fe, are keen hunters. For centuries, falconry has been the passionate pastime of the Iberian aristocracy, both Christian and Moorish.

I collect my horse, Tinto, and go to the falcons' mews, where I tie him outside.

It is dark and cool inside so that the hunting-birds are comfortable. A dozen hawks and falcons rest on their perches. When I enter, one or two stretch and flap their wings, jingling the bells of the jesses, the long leather leashes on their legs. Most of them continue to doze, with feathers fluffed out.

I greet the falconer, Moises Sanchez. Jewish boys like Moises work in camp support jobs, for all able-bodied Christian men of fighting age are in the army. Moises is in his teens, and one of Juan's best friends.

"Flechita is well?" I ask. My own hunting falcon, a peregrine whose name translates to 'Little Arrow' in English, hears my voice and starts a happy, bobbing dance on her perch. I kiss the feathers on the top of her head.

There is a rigid, unbreakable hierarchy in falconry. Small peregrines like Flechita are allocated to young aristocrats; noblemen fly the bigger hawks, and only the king, the queen, or a Moorish sultan can fly the largest breeds of falcon or an eagle.

Moises smiles. "Flechita is very well, as you can see. Are you hunting today? Where is your brother?"

"I'm going by myself. Juan's busy."

"Do you think you should go out alone today, with the army on the move? Your mother will worry. I'll come with you, after I finish feeding the birds." Moises carefully counts out cubes of freshly-killed rabbit meat on a pair of scales. The birds need precise amounts of food to keep them fit for hunting.

"You don't need to come with me. I won't go far." I stroke

Flechita's soft breast feathers, and she cocks her head to one side, making soft whistling sounds.

"Well, don't stray from the road, and keep within sight of the fort."

"Of course."

Moises watches me with Flechita. "You have a way with falcons," he admires my rapport with her.

"That's because of my patron saint, *San Juan Evangelista*. Saint John the Evangelist. His sign is the sign of the eagle. San Juan wrote the gospel and the Book of Revelation, and I'm sure that the eagle helped him. They say San Juan is the patron saint of writers, but I'm sure he's the patron of falcons, too."

Moises sets a brass weight on the scales to balance another ration of meat. These scales are used for measuring gold, but falcons are equally valuable.

I teasingly reach out with one finger to tip the balance, withdrawing before I touch it. "All the saints and apostles have their special symbols. Saint Peter has his keys. Saint James, *Santiago*, has his scallop shell."

"Ah, of course. I've seen the statues in your church."

"Don't you have saints in the synagog, Moises?"

"No, we have prophets. And they are in our book, not made into statues."

"Oh, we have everything. Books, prophets, saints and statues. My great-grandmother was Jewish, and she became a *converso*, so she could have it all."

"I know," he says dryly. *She had it all, including the King of Aragon.*

I watch Moises carefully scrape the cubes of meat from the scales into a jade-green ceramic bowl. I follow him as he walks down the line of birds. He stops at the end. This big falcon is the most fabulous creature I've ever seen, with its classic hook of razor-sharp beak, plumage gleaming like polished steel and its cold, golden stare. Its arrogant, intelligent expression is like the carved eagle of San Juan, the wings outstretched against the evangelist's robes, in the Cathedral of Seville.

"A new one!" I exclaim.

Moises steps protectively in front of me. "She just arrived last week. Careful, stay back. Her name is Mumtaz, and she's a Saker falcon."

Moises feeds her cubes of meat, mindful of the tips of his fingers. Mumtaz snatches the pieces with her sharp beak. "She is a gift to your mother, from the Emir of Almeria."

Almeria is the Moorish province on the Mediterranean east coast of Spain. Almeria, once an ally of the Moorish Kingdom of Granada, surrendered and signed a truce with us Christians. The Emir, in return for peace, agreed to accept the Christian Kingdom of Castile, and my mother, the queen, as his overlord and new ally. The Saker falcon is a priceless gift.

"Has Mama hunted her yet?"

"No, the queen has no time for hunting now. I've taken Mumtaz out, and she kills quickly and cleanly. When she sees her prey, she's like a bolt shot from a crossbow."

"I'd like to try her."

"Perhaps not yet, Lady Juana," Moises says diplomatically. He and I both know the rules of falconry. I am not allowed to fly this calibre of bird. "Mumtaz is still getting used to her new home with us. If she gets upset, she might fly back to Almeria! Besides, I think it will rain. Falcons get restless when there's a storm."

24

I shrug. I pick up Mumtaz's leather hunting hood and toy with it.

"I thought I'd hunt for partridges today. They are Papa's favourite, and I could send them to him, for dinner at his new headquarters." I pull on the heavy leather gauntlet where my falcon will perch on my forearm.

"I'll get Flechita ready for you," Moises says. "But first, some fresh water for Mumtaz." He hefts an empty ceramic water pitcher to his shoulder, and goes outside to the well.

As soon as he's gone, I put the leather hunting hood over Mumtaz's head and eyes – which silences her and makes her docile – and raise her from her perch onto my gauntlet. My arm sags unexpectedly with her weight. She is heavier than I thought, compared with little Flechita. I feel Mumtaz's sharp talons gripping through the leather.

I rush from the mews, with a guilty look back at Flechita, who chirrups to attract my attention. I see Flechita trying to follow me, tugging against the restraint of her jesses, the tiny bells ringing in protest at her abandonment.

I quickly untie my horse and lead him around the side of the building, out of sight of Moises. There I use a mounting block to step up carefully into the saddle, keeping Mumtaz steady. I look around. There is no one to see me. Juan and I have a secret way out of the fort that avoids the sentries posted at the main gate.

I leave the security of Fort Santa Fe behind me, following a narrow goat track through the wild country. This trail is a short distance from the new military road to Granada, running parallel to it for several miles. The military road is where my father and Lord Sales and the soldiers marched yesterday, where the oxen hauled the great cannons to the siege of the City of Granada, and where the mule trains carry supplies. It is the road our army engineers built this summer at a terrible cost in men and draft animals. It cuts through the steepest mountains where there had never been a road, and where the Moorish defenders of the City of Granada believed it was impossible to build one. It stretches thirty-five miles from Fort Santa Fe to the gates of the Alhambra.

✠

In the land of southern Spain that we Christians call Andalucia, and the Moors call Al-Andalus, the long, dry months of summer burn with a furnace-heavy heat that sears the lungs with every breath; the short months of winter are cold and wet, with driving rain that drowns the land. What astonishes foreigners is how fast the change between the dry season and rainy season falls, within hours of a single day, like a sword of Toledo steel slashing through silk.

King Fernando's troops, with Lord Sales and his English archers, and the priests with the Silver Cross, set up their new headquarters within sight of Granada. The sun is blisteringly hot, and the men and horses run with sweat. There has been no rain since May; summer and autumn are hotter and drier than any in living memory, and within the besieged City of Granada the Muslim *imams* pray for the winter rains to begin.

Granada is crowded with refugees from surrounding Moorish farms and villages destroyed by Christian raids. Rich Arab merchant families from Malaga, Ronda and Almeria, who fled the Christian takeovers of their cities, add to the press of those sheltering behind the city walls. Yet Granada remains in good order, with the remaining food and water carefully rationed. From the watchtowers on the walls of the Alhambra, the Moors can see the Christian army encamped.

Black thunderclouds gather. Shadows sweep like a dark velvet cover over the land and the big war mastiffs with the Christian army growl as they sense the promise of rain. The artillery men aim the mouths of their cannons toward the Alhambra's walls, waiting for the order to fire.

King Fernando sends a message to the Moorish King Boabdil. *We have cut off your food supplies. Our army surrounds the City of Granada. Agree to an honorable surrender and be spared, or else our cannons will bombard the walls, and our soldiers will storm your city, and no mercy will be shown in battle. The choice is yours.*

There is no reply. The messenger returns empty-handed.

King Fernando turns to Lord Sales "Why do you think King Boabil is refusing to talk terms?"

"He's probably arguing with fanatics inside his court. Rather than surrender, some will want to destroy Granada and die fighting."

"Surely not King Boabdil. He's a reasonable young man, more poet than warrior. I met him once. We captured him during a skirmish, nearly eight years ago. His mother – she's formidable – paid a huge ransom for his safe return."

Edmund Sales stares at the dark clouds over the Sierra Nevada mountains. "I think the Moors pray for the return of the rainy season. They're stalling for time. Rain is bad news for us. We'll have a devil of a time getting mule trains through the mountains and keeping the gunpowder dry for the cannons. And even my best English archers can't fire with wet bowstrings."

✠

I feel Mumtaz tremble on my arm as she senses the weather shifting. I ride over a series of small hills for nearly two miles. The sky above me is half-covered with rolling dark clouds, which I hope to outrun; I leave the trail and ride into unfamiliar countryside. The world turns to twilight and my eyes adjust slowly to the shadowland I travel through, determined to find quarry at which to fly Mumtaz.

A gust of wind blows my broad-brimmed hat away and my hair is coming loose, whipping across my face as the wind rises. The red ribbon with which I had tied my hair flies away; I can't grab the hat or the ribbon without upsetting Mumtaz or dropping the reins. I bite my lip in regret, for the ribbon was a birthday gift to me from Lord Sales.

The black clouds cover the entire sky now, and my horse, Tinto, tosses his head restlessly when I rein to a halt. I can hear echoing sounds in the distance and can't tell if it is the army siege cannons, or thunder.

Then I see movement in the shallow valley below me: game birds – quarry at last! *This is even better than partridges, I rejoice, forgetting the weather. These are giant bustards.*

There are five of these, as large as swans and running like ostriches on their long legs, their necks stretched out as they strain to raise their heavy bodies into the air, their wings flapping. *A bustard will make a royal feast for Papa's dinner, I think triumphantly, Mumtaz is big enough to kill one.* My little peregrine

Flechita, proven killer of small partridges, would not have the size or strength to bring down a giant bustard.

I sweep off Mumtaz's hood; she sees her prey and launches herself from my gauntlet. True to her killing style, the Saker falcon does not fly up into the sky to gain a vantage point, but shoots straight after her quarry.

The bustards struggle for height, skimming just above the dried yellow grass until their wing-beats lift them high enough to brush the tops of the wild olive trees. Mumtaz soars over the first hill and gains rapidly on the last bustard, which swerves to avoid her talons. My own spirit flies with the falcon as she closes on her prey. They bank over a second hill, with Mumtaz only a hand's breadth behind. My heart stops as they vanish from my sight.

I anxiously snatch Tinto's reins and gallop through a grove of cork oak trees to the top of the ridge. I see nothing. There are no bustards, there is no sign of Mumtaz, and I don't recognise any of the countryside. Then thick, oily drops of water strike my face like lead shot.

I flinch as a great crack of thunder breaks the sky apart and the rain spills from the heavens like a waterfall over a cliff. The pent-up, long awaited rain of Andalucia falls in a powerful torrent. It streams into my eyes and hammers my bare head so hard it hurts.

I slither out of the wet saddle, soothing Tinto, and splash through the puddles, my eyes searching the ground. If Mumtaz has caught the bustard, she will be down, hunched over her prey, great wings outstretched to guard it.

I feel panic rising and I clutch Mumtaz's leather helmet, with its rain-soaked crest of coloured feathers.

Lightning flashes through the air; I jump when it strikes the cork oak tree next to me. The temperature plummets, and I shiver. My riding cloak is drenched through and my wet blouse sticks to my skin, as if pressed by the cold hands of a witch.

I close my eyes and pray to San Juan, then I cuff the rain from my face to see the outline of a cave mouth in the cliff ahead of me. I tug Tinto's reins to pull him forward. We can shelter in the cave until the worst of the storm is over.

My ears ring from the peals of thunder, and I can't see through the pouring rain. I bow my head and keep my eyes focused on the ground at my feet, searching for any sign of Mumtaz.

Tinto jerks at the reins, whinnying in fear, and I feel two heavy hands on my shoulders. I look up. In front of me is a thick-set man, his head swathed in a grey turban, his face dark and bearded.

"What are you doing here, little one?" He speaks in the Andalucian Arab patois. Rainwater drips from his bushy eyebrows and wet turban.

I force myself to swallow my fear, and I reply in the same dialect. "Hunting. I've lost my new falcon." My hands shake and I drop Mumtaz's beautiful leather helmet to the muddy ground.

A second Moor comes splashing through the puddles, his robe sodden with rain. "What's this, Musa?"

"A girl. A Christian girl." He grabs the cross on a gold chain that I wear around my neck.

I pull the cross away from him and hiss in anger. He laughs and takes Tinto's reins.

"A spirited little thing, aren't you?" He crouches down so his face is level with mine. One of his front teeth is missing. "You're pretty, too. Will someone pay to ransom you? Or we could sell you as a slave. The sultan in Morocco pays a lot of gold for pretty girls."

"Come on, Musa, let's just get her out of the rain. Take her to the cave."

Sheltering in the cave, I see eight horses tethered, with Moorish bridles and saddles and fringed saddlecloths. I see a servant puffing life into a fire of wet kindling, and around the spluttering flames six richly-dressed men sit in a circle.

"My Lord, we have found a girl," my captor says as we enter the cave.

"What? Here? Alone?"

"She says she is 'hunting'."

"Come here, child. Don't be afraid." The young man who beckons to me speaks in perfect Castilian Spanish. He wears a shimmering, emerald-green silk cloak, the edges richly embroidered in gold thread. His snowy white turban is pinned with a large ruby set in gold, which reflects the heart of the fire.

My tongue goes dry and sticks to the roof of my mouth. I know there are good Moors, friends and allies, like Juan's Sufi music teacher and the masters of Hispano-Arab poetry at my parents' court. Juan and I grew up with the children of the Moorish architects who live in Seville and Cordoba. I met the proud independent Moorish Emirs and their entourages who came to agree peace terms with my parents. But I also know – warnings from my mother ringing in my ears – that there are

31

Muslim fanatics who enslave or kill any Christian they can capture.

"What are you hunting?" the young man, apparently their commander, asks me in a kind voice. He is seated on a fine carpet and pats the empty space next to him. He looks to be in his mid-twenties in age and is very handsome, with a light-brown beard and dark eyes outlined in kohl. He dismisses the two men who brought me into the cave. They go, reluctantly leaving the circle of firelight, back out into the lashing rain to stand guard.

My hopes rise. "I'm trying a new falcon. She nearly caught a great bustard, then the storm hit and I can't find her."

"Your falcon almost caught a great bustard? Truly? A young girl like you must be flying a peregrine. Yet you tried to catch a bustard with a little peregrine?"

"Mumtaz is a Saker falcon," I say in a small voice.

The turbaned heads around the campfire swing toward me in unison.

"A Saker?" Someone chuckles to his companions. "Children don't hunt with Sakers." They all know that only the most exalted royalty hunt with such a bird.

The commander silences his officers with a graceful wave of his hand and looks intently at me. "We, too, have been hunting," he says companionably. "I find freedom in hunting. As you do, perhaps?" He nods toward their horses, their lances, their scimitars and the hooded big falcons with their keeper. I don't see Mumtaz among their birds.

As the fire takes hold of the wood, it casts more light on the commander's face. The other men whisper among themselves, and my sharp ears catch one exchange, "All hell breaking loose around us in the city, and he decides to go hunting."

A servant adds more small branches to the fire and sprinkles a handful of fragrant incense onto the glowing embers.

"Are you getting warmer?" the commander asks me, as I continue to shiver. "Here, give Ahmed your wet cloak to dry out by the fire, and take mine." He wraps the lovely soft folds around my shoulders. "Who are you, child? Where is your family?"

"I am Juana de Trastamara. My family lives at Santa Fe." I snuggle into the perfumed warmth of the cloak. The commander looks into my face, searching my features. I see the others' eyes signaling one to the other.

One man exclaims, "*Inshallah*, she must be one of the royal children. What a stroke of luck! We can keep her for ransom. Our hunting party has captured the best quarry God could send us."

The commander strokes his beard, stares into the fire and asks his officers for their opinions. I remain as still and large-eyed as a gazelle fawn in a pride of lions.

I know by their clothing and their accents that these men are Moors, Spanish Muslims. A young officer speaks first, saying eagerly to the commander, "It's obvious to me. She's a chessboard pawn, to be used to bargain with King Fernando. This is our best chance to break the siege."

An older man disagrees. A scar runs through his neatly-trimmed grey beard; his blue silk turban is tied with an elaborate knot and tassel. He speaks with the resonant voice of a poet. "My Lord, the noblest gesture would be to return the child without any ransom demand at all. It's our code of chivalry, for she is a non-combatant."

A harsh voice, in the Arab accent of a country far away, echoes from the back of the cave. "It's no use sitting around arguing about her." A tall thin older man stalks into the circle of firelight. He reminds me of a giant bat, unfurling the sleeves of his rusty black robe. His turban is threadbare and black, the badge of a foreign *jihadi*. "Daughters are worthless to a king."

I strain to understand him, for although I know the Andalucian Arabic patois, this man is different. He must be one of the thousands of foreign Arab warriors, called *jihadis*, who have flooded into Andalucia from the far shores of the Mediterranean to fight against us in the Granada War. He has a long thin grey beard, reaching down his chest, which he claws at as he speaks. "If only you had captured the king's son."

The Spanish Moors lower their eyes.

The poet with the elaborate turban shakes his head "No, you foreigners do not understand this country. The Kingdom of Aragon is ruled by King Fernando, but the Kingdom of Castile is ruled by his wife, separately. Queen Isabel reigns by right of her birth and by her own sword. Castile's throne goes first to her son, then her daughters follow her in the line of succession." I see the *jihadi* stare at me with new interest. "Then give me the girl," he says to the commander.

The officers shift uncomfortably and someone coughs. I know that the Spanish Moors find these foreign *jihadis* alien to our Andalucian customs. I remembered when the Emir of Almeria conferred with my parents, he spoke of how deeply the Spanish Moors resent the pious airs and strident demands of these stark fundamentalists, who beat the hilts of their sabers at the mosque doors of Granada to announce they have come to save the Spanish Moors from the Spanish Christians. "We feel," the Emir of Almeria said, "that we have more in common with our Spanish Christian adversaries than we do with these alien foreigners."

There is a binding thread that runs though the souls of those born and raised in Spain, whether Muslim, Christian, or Jewish. For 700 years, we have shared this same land, under respective rulers who upheld the *conviviencia*, which translates as 'the living together.'

No matter how fiercely we fight among ourselves, Spanish Muslims, Spanish Christians and Spanish Jews know in our hearts that we are all Iberians, born with the same strengths and forged in the same southern fires, with unbreakable bonds of place and *pueblo* and family. We hold fast to codes of pride and honour, and a friendship once made is a friendship for life. We know that Iberia makes us different from those who come from the world outside the peninsula.

Listening to the *jihadi's* words, I edge closer to the young commander's side. I find his scent comfortingly familiar, similar to my father's, of horses and leather and wild lavender. Then I catch a scent that confuses me: his breath carries the faint, sour tang of wine, of a man who drank too much the night before. *But devout Muslims don't drink, I think. I wonder why he would need the solace of wine's forgetfulness?*

He looks reassuringly at me. The great ruby in his turban glows. He raises his right hand and the large emerald in his ring sparkles. "No, Muktada Bin Kadim," the commander says to the *jihadi*. "You will not take her. I am the one who will decide her fate."

"I am your guest, and I respect your wishes." The stranger's words drip like honeycomb, sliced with a razor edge of resentment.

The commander rises. "When the storm ends, I will escort the girl back to the Christian army road. Once she is there, I will free her to ride back to her own people."

The late afternoon sun dissolves the rainclouds and throws a cloth of gold *mantilla* over the countryside. The highest peaks of the Sierra Nevada mountains are left blazing white, for on the summit the rain has fallen as the first snow of winter.

The Moorish commander and his entourage collect their horses and falcons, and the servant lifts me onto my own mount. My nearly-dry riding cape is returned to me, and I reluctantly hand back the commander's splendid green cloak.

When we leave the cave, our horses pick their way carefully over the slippery, wet ground, under the dripping trees. I see the old *jihadi* lingering behind, slowing his horse to be the last one.

When we reach the *dehesa*, the open countryside studded with great oak trees, we pick up the pace, and I canter Tinto, stirrup to stirrup, alongside the commander's black stallion. We ride through a series of hills, each valley hidden from the next like folds in wrinkled fabric.

Several times we have to divert to find a longer way around *arroyos*, which had been dry dusty hollows all summer and now foam with raging currents of floodwater. We ease our horses down a steep path, through clumps of spiky juniper and duck under the the low-hanging branches of a massive cork oak tree. The commander leans out from his saddle and touches the cork bark, which is as thick and fissured as a sea sponge.

"Here it is, the turn for the Christian road."

The commander and I move slightly ahead of the others. He stops, raises his eyes and stares at the snow-clad Sierra Nevada mountains in the distance.

"I remember, when I was a little boy, my nurse telling me romantic stories of long-ago days. The one I liked best was the story of the Moorish emir who marries a Christian princess from the north of Spain. But the princess wept with sadness – even in the beautiful Alhambra – because she missed the winter snows of her homeland."

"I know that story," I say. "I heard it from my nurse,too. I love the stories of the days of El Cid."

"And how did your nurse's story end, little one?"

"The Moorish emir couldn't bear his Christian wife being unhappy. He ordered his gardeners to plant hundreds of almond trees below her palace window. In the spring, the almond trees were covered in white blossom, just like snow. The princess saw it and was delighted with the sight and with how much her husband loved her, and the two of them were blessed with great happiness together."

He nods. "The story I learned was the same."

His men gather around us, by the Christian army road that slices like a fresh axe wound through the mountains, from Fort Santa Fe to the City of Granada.

The commander nods in the direction I should take, the road west.

"Go with God, my little Lady Juana. Give my regards to your worthy father and mother."

"I will. But who shall I say sends them greetings?"

His fingertips gracefully touch first his heart, then his lips and then his forehead, ending with his palm outstretched toward me in the traditional Moorish salute. His eyes never leave mine.

"Boabdil, the King of Granada."

Stunned, I watch as they wheel their horses and gallop east toward the City of Granada. They avoid the Christian road, and none of them looks back.

I turn Tinto onto the road to Santa Fe. In several places the rain has washed the surface away into deep gullies and treacherous potholes, and I think of my father and his army and the oxen pulling the cannons over this same road when it was still dry and hard.

*War. I've lived my entire life in the shadow of the Granada War. Now I have met the enemy of my father and mother, face-to-face.* I discover he and I both cherish the same romantic tale of centuries past, the time of the Spanish *conviviencia*, the 'living together' of Muslim, Jew, and Christian. It was a time when love could cross the barriers of religion and opposing kingdoms. *Could it happen again now?*

After seven or eight paces, I stop and stare at the hills where King Boabdil has disappeared. A new thought enters my head. *Marriage.* Before, it was all grown-ups talk, and I ignored it. My eldest sister Isabella will be married sometime soon, she's betrothed to the King of Portugal, and they say that will bind Castile's Western neighbour to us.

But what of Castile's Southern neighbour, the Moorish

Kingdom of Granada? *It was once the custom to arrange royal marriages across religious lines. But this changed over the centuries, and I wonder if my parents would ever consider – even for a moment – a marriage contract to end the Granada War.*

I sigh and remember each detail of meeting King Boabdil in the cave. *What might it be like to be betrothed to him?* My heart beats quicker. I know that something warmed me even more than the campfire: being close to him.

✠

I notice Tinto beginning to limp, and I slide out of the saddle to discover why. His left fore hoof has picked up a stone, and I can't dislodge it with my fingers. I begin, on foot, to lead him slowly back to Fort Santa Fe. I sing to him, to keep up his spirits, and my own. I'm going to be in trouble when I get back to the Fort, and at this rate, with a lame horse, it will be after dark. *No partridges or a bustard to send to my father for his dinner – I feel I've let him down. I've lost my mother's falcon, and dread her reaction. I almost wish King Boabdil had kept me captive.*

Then on the road ahead, I see two figures riding toward me at the gallop. One waves his hat and shouts my name. I call back, "Juan, Juan, it's me!" My brother has found me.

In the joy of reunion, we do not see someone watching us from the shadows. A black-robed man on horseback who keeps out of sight, hovering like a malign shadow, flitting bat-like behind the oak trees and tumbled boulders.

✠

Juan jumps from his horse to hug me and Moises canters up behind him, and gathers our horses.

"Thank God you're safe – we've been looking everywhere for you. We found your hat, miles back, and thought you might have been thrown."

My brother holds me close, and I feel his clothes are soaking wet from the rain and his body shivers with cold.

I see Moises' face, hurt and angry.

"I lost Mama's Saker falcon," I tell him, my voice quivering. "I lost Mumtaz. I'm so sorry I took her, Moises, I'm so sorry."

I bury my head against my brother's shoulder. "Mama will be so angry, Juan."

"Don't worry. I'll take care of you. I'll take the blame. Mama never gets angry at me for anything."

Juan looks at Moises. "Don't tell the queen about Juana and the falcon. I'll say I took Mumtaz hunting without your permission, and she flew away."

"As you wish, Don Juan."

I can see that he's afraid that he might lose his job as royal falconer. Or worse.

Juan smooths my hair. "You're almost dry, did you find shelter from the storm?"

I nod. "In a cave in the hills. Then coming home, Tinto went lame."

Juan expertly runs a hand down the horse's left foreleg, lifting it to check the hoof. He uses his knife to pry the embedded stone lose. "Just a bruise. He'll be all right, if he goes very slowly. Moises, would you please lead Juana's horse back to the fort?"

"By myself?" Moises is uneasy. "It's almost dark now. What are you going to do?"

"Juana will ride double with me. We'll go faster and send guards to escort you safely home." Juan scoops me up to ride pillion behind his saddle.

"And what happens to me when the queen finds out Mumtaz is missing? You say you'll take the blame, but it's her best falcon. A gift from the Emir of Almeria!"

"Don't worry, my friend. Nothing will happen, I swear it on the Crown of the Holy Virgin," my brother says.

Moises rolls his eyes heavenward. He gets back in the saddle, making clicking sounds to encourage Tinto to follow with leading reins. Moises scans the treetops and the wet ground for signs of the missing falcon.

My brother puts his horse into a trot and we leave Moises behind.

"How did you find me?" I ask Juan, clasping my arms tighter around his waist.

"We found your trail, leading out of the fort before the rain started. We followed Tinto's hoofprints through the *dehesa*. Moises found your hat, then the storm broke, and the rain washed out your tracks."

"Did you find my red ribbon, the one Lord Sales gave me?"

"No, the wind must have blown it away. What a storm!" My brother shivers. "I was so worried about you out here alone. First the rain – we got soaked – and then we got pelted by hailstones as big as pigeons' eggs."

The horse slips through a pool of mud and I shift my weight to keep my balance.

"I'm sorry I took Mumtaz. I didn't think about poor Moises. He's so worried."

"Moises is Jewish. He's always worried about something." Juan makes a joke, trying to lighten my mood. "You worry too much, Juana."

"Maybe I'm more Jewish than you think. Like Great-Grandmother Merina."

"Great-Grandmother Merina became a Christian, remember?"

"Do you think it's easy for people to change religions?"

"Maybe not easy, but it can be done. That's why we pray and Mama keeps having Masses said. So that the Jews and the Moors will change and become Christians, just like us."

"Then why doesn't Moises become a Christian?"

Juan is silent; I can tell he's thinking. I feel his heart beating as I hug closer to him for balance. "I don't know," he says at last. "I don't know."

I hug him tighter. His clothes are wet through, and he feels unnaturally cold. "There's something else about the cave," I half-whisper in his ear, and I tell him about the Moors I encountered there.

He stops the horse and twists in the saddle to stare into my face in disbelief.

I continue nervously. "The commander I met, the good Moor, said he was the King of Granada. It was Boabdil himself. He was kind, and he took me back to the road and let me go. He even told me to send his greetings to Mama and Papa."

Juan shakes his head. "Did this really happen to you, or is it one of your stories?"

"It's real. Believe me."

"Juana, I said I'd come with you to take our falcons hunting, and you didn't wait for me. And look what happened! Holy Mother, what if the Moors kept you for ransom?" His voice darkens. "You know the Moors capture Christians and make them slaves. We saw them at Malaga."

"I remember," I shudder. At Malaga, four years ago, I saw hundreds of young Christian women and boys chained up, ready to be shipped off to the slave markets overseas. Our Christian army had taken the Moors' main seaport city, Malaga, with a naval blockade – which is why the Christian slaves were trapped there.

I close my eyes and see them again: slaves. For hundreds of years, the slave trade has been a profitable enterprise for the Kingdom of Granada. The Moors attack Spanish Christian villages to round up prisoners for slaves; sometimes, under a truce, the raids are suspended. The Granada War started twelve years ago when the Moors broke the treaty and began the slave raids again. They sell the captive Spanish Christians overseas to Morocco and Cairo and Constantinople; the slave traders take the most beautiful young women and girls, who fetch the highest prices. The raiders also take young boys; the most intelligent and appealing ones to be castrated and sold as eunuchs.

The strongest Christian young men are not castrated, but forcibly converted to Islam and sold to foreign sultans to serve in the elite royal palace guards. The Jannisary Regiment at the Topkapi Palace in Constantinople is made up of such men.

I remembered Malaga, when our Christian army besieged the city and blockaded the port. The Moorish commander sent my father an ultimatum: end the siege of Malaga and take your army away now, or else we kill the Christian captives we hold.

My father replied that if the enslaved Christians were harmed, he would raze every single building and kill every last Moor in Malaga.

So Malaga surrendered to my parents. The Christian slaves were herded out, barely alive, by their Moorish jailers. I saw my mother weep, as she helped the doctors and nursing nuns bath the captives' wounds.

My mother ordered the heavy iron slave manacles to be struck off their bleeding wrists and ankles. She commanded that the manacles and slave chains were to be sent to Toledo, to the Monastery of San Juan de los Reyes. There, they hang on the church walls, a reminder and a thanksgiving for deliverance of her people. She said it would be a sign to the world that all Spanish Christian men and women would forever live free.

Juan notices how quiet I have become, thinking of Malaga. He nudges me back to the present. "Maybe this Moorish commander from the cave really isn't King Boabdil," he says in a lighter tone. "Maybe he's an outlaw who found you, and pretended to be someone important."

"Oh no, I'm sure it is King Boabdil. Why, if you could have seen his clothes, his horse, the great ruby he wore in his turban and his emerald ring!"

Juan's teeth chatter with cold when he replies. "Mama has enough worries with the war. This story about King Boabdil – if it was him – and your almost being taken captive will only upset her more. Don't tell Mama about it, not yet. Let me talk to her first."

I remain silent.

"Promise?" Juan asks.

"I promise. Not a word to anyone."

Juan starts to reply, but then he begins to cough. We see Fort Santa Fe ahead of us, with torches being lit on the perimeter.

On the outskirts of the fort, near the latrines and rubbish dumps, we ride through the corrals and pens holding the beasts for slaughter. There are herds of hundreds of cattle and sheep, goats and pigs, to feed the fort and the army. Meat is our main source of food, because we are a people always on the move, so the animals are driven on the hoof to where they are needed.

The slaughtermen and butchers are working by flaming braziers into the evening, for the army needs food constantly and the cooler weather signals the *matanza*, the pig-killing. I see the firelight flickering on the red face of the master-butcher, arms thick as the hams that hang on a pole behind him. The muscles of his naked chest ripple as he dismembers the carcass of a large pig, the body splayed in a crude, wooden cradle.

The butcher's forearms are covered in blood, as he slices his large knife through flesh and sinew. On the ground beside him is a big, rough, glazed pottery bowl with the pig's intestines, coils of purple and red, glistening wetly in the firelight, buzzing with drowsy flies and waiting to be washed out and made into *morcilla* – blood sausages. The stench of the slaughtered pig makes Juan's horse skitter nervously, rolling its eyes and blowing loudly through its nostrils.

The butcher looks up from his work and his face breaks into a smile when he recognises us. "Don Juan, Lady Juana!" he waves the butchering knife in the air in greeting. "Where have you been? Your mother is looking everywhere for you."

He puts two bloody fingers into his mouth, whistles loudly and a royal page comes running toward us. He is one of the young couriers who carry the queen's messages throughout the fort.

The page wrinkles his nose at the smell. He makes a small bow to us. "The queen, your mother, wishes to see you immediately. She's in the chapel, at evening Mass, with your sisters."

"Thank you," Juan says. "We'll join them." His voice takes on a new tone, one of command, and he tells the page, "Would you please see that two mounted guards are sent to the military road? They need to find Moises Sanchez and escort him home. Moises is leading my sister's lame horse and he's some way behind us. And tell the guards to bring Moises back through the main gate, not through here." He gestures at the pork butchery.

The master-butcher nods in understanding sympathy. Jews and Muslims don't like anything to do with pigs.

✠

When Juan and Juana leave, the master-butcher returns to his work, singing an out-of-tune ribald ballad as he breaks apart the carcass. He has known Juan and Juana since they were babies, having served the queen and king throughout the Granada War.

"What a noise you're making! You call that singing? It sounds more like a stuck pig," a laughing voice calls from the darkness. Into the circle of light cast by the brazier walks a sentry, prodding a prisoner in front of him.

"Look what I found skulking outside the fort," the soldier says proudly, jabbing his sword-tip in the small of the prisoner's back to urge him closer to the firelight.

The prisoner is a tall, thin older man, with a long beard nearly to his waist. He is dressed in a threadbare black robe and black turban.

"He had a horse with him, but it ran off when I pulled him from the saddle," the soldier says, eyeing the hams hung behind butcher. "Funny, though. This fellow didn't put up any fight at all."

The prisoner recoils in horror at the sight and smell of the butchered pig, and the soldier chuckles.

"Unclean, eh?" the soldier asks him. "You don't know what you're missing. I love pork." He sniffs appreciatively and taps the bowl of intestines with the toe of his boot. "You making your *morcilla* sausages, Paco?"

The butcher nods. "Special request from the English Lord Sales. The English love sausages."

"Save some for me," the soldier winks. "*Morcilla* for breakfast tomorrow, there's a treat. Maybe the old boy here will have some too, if he decides to become a Christian."

Pork is the meat that divides the Spanish. The Spanish Christians eat pork; Spanish Muslims and Spanish Jews will not touch it. Eating pork is used by the Inquisition to test *conversos*. If a former Jew or Muslim professes to be true Christian, the feast after the baptism includes thick, fat-streaked slices of smoked *jamon*, and coils of rich sausages, *morcilla* and *chorizo*.

"I'm taking this fellow to the captain of the guard. The old boy only speaks Arabic. I think I've got his name, though:

Muktada." The soldier grins at his charge. "Do you want to become a Christian, Muktada?"

The prisoner draws back his robes to avoid any stray splashes of pig's blood.

"I don't believe him," the butcher says.

"Come on, Paco. The queen is always praying and having Masses said for the conversion of Jews and Muslims. Maybe we're going to see some results at last."

The soldier takes the old man by the arm. "There are more and more Moorish deserters giving themselves up. The Moors are tired of this war, more tired then we are. And hungrier." The soldier scratches his stomach. Tucked into his belt is the curved, Arabic dagger, taken when he disarmed his prisoner.

"The captain says, if Moors surrender to us, just keep them under guard the first night. Then if the captain thinks they can be trusted, we set them to work repairing the road or herding animals."

The butcher makes a gesture of eating a piece of pork he's just cut, and points toward the prisoner.

The old man gasps as if he would be sick.

"Don't worry," Paco says cheerfully. "It's lamb stew for your dinner tonight. No *morcilla* until after the baptism."

✠

Juan and I dismount and run to meet our mother and sisters, who are returning to the family quarters after the evening Mass. A page leads them through the narrow street, holding a lighted lantern.

Little Catalina rushes up to take my hand, prattling away

48

happily. Over my baby sister's chatter, I hear Juan telling Mama that after he had finished dispatching the mule trains, he and I had gone hunting. A coughing fit interrupts him, and Mama puts a hand to Juan's forehead.

"Your clothes are wet, and your face feels like ice," she says with a worried frown.

"It's nothing, Mama. I got caught in the rain." He bows his head. "I'm sorry, Mama. I took your new Saker falcon hunting. She flew away, and I can't find her."

"Oh, Juan, that falcon was a gift from the Emir of Almeria. Why did Moises let you take her?"

"It wasn't his Moises's fault, Mama. He told me not to, but I did it anyway. Then the storm came and I lost Mumtaz. Then Juana's horse bolted and we got separated."

My mother frowns at me. *Juana is always the one at the centre whenever there is trouble.*

"Juana found a cave to shelter in, but I kept looking for Mumtaz."

Our mother's disappointment over the falcon is swept away by her anxiety over Juan's health. She rushes us back to our quarters and orders my brother to bed, with a brazier brought to warm his room.

The rain falls again that night. Over the pounding of rain on the roof tiles I can hear Juan coughing in his room next door. Mama rises several times in the night to go to him, and in the morning she asks Father Cisneros to say a special Mass and pray to the Virgin and to San Juan for my brother's recovery.

*Juan is strong and healthy,* I tell myself, *he just caught a cold. Surely he will shake it off.*

Juan does not improve. The next day, he is struck with a raging fever and then chills. Mama tells me and my sisters not to disturb him, and she summons our family's Jewish doctor, Don Lorenzo Badoc.

The doctor prepares a special hot herbal broth for Juan to drink, but nothing seems to relieve the congestion in his lungs. I join my sisters in the chapel to pray. Even Father Cisneros looks worried. After evening Mass, Mama allows me and my sisters into Juan's room to kiss him goodnight. His eyes are bright with pain and his throat hurts too much to talk to me. My sisters and I tiptoe back to own room, but Mama remains at his bedside with Doctor Badoc and Father Cisneros.

My eldest sister Isabella blows out the candle and our room is dark. There is no happy chatter among my sisters that night from our respective beds. I feel their accusing silence aimed directly at me. They think it's my fault that Juan is ill.

I sigh loudly, and get rebuked by Isabella. "So, 'Diana the Huntress', you hid in a dry cave while poor Juan was out in the storm looking for that stupid bird." Isabella sarcastically taunts me with the name 'Diana the Huntress,' the pagan goddess of the chase. Isabella is like a second, sterner, mother to us, her younger siblings. I try to ignore her.

But I cannot ignore the terrible sounds of my brother's coughing in the next room. A long stretch of silence spins out into the darkness, and I fear that ominous quiet means death. Then I hear Juan coughing again, the broken rasps of his struggle to force air into his lungs. Then silence. And again, the racking, wrenching coughs.

That night haunts me for years to come. I am on the edge of the abyss. *This is the terror of my nightmare, the foreboding nightmare of the warship in the great storm, with Juan clinging to the rail, clinging to life.* I pray that Juan can hold on. There is no Father Adrian here, as in my nightmare, to break my brother's hands and send him plummeting into the dark sea of death.

My life and Juan's life are linked together. I share my brother's lessons, for Juan insisted that I be allowed to join him; our busy parents agreed to his request. It is difficult for them to refuse Juan anything. Juan and I study together under the finest tutors of poetry, music, philosophy, languages, religion; we train under the greatest masters of riding and swordsmanship. Juan and I love both music best; our brightest moments together are when Juan composes his own songs to play on the guitar and I dance in accompaniment.

But now, through the darkness comes the blinding fear of losing my beloved brother forever to death. My heart hammers. *Everything is my fault,* I berate myself. *I took the Saker falcon. It is my fault that Juan caught cold trying to find me.* I lay awake under my blanket, tossing with anxiety. I try to bury my head under my pillow to muffle the sound of my brother's coughing.

But I can still hear sounds from my brother's room. Doctor Badoc, his voice tense with urgency, says something to my mother. I raise my head to hear the servants' slippered feet whispering over the woven grass floor mats, and my mother summoning her courier.

"Take this letter to King Fernando at the front line at Granada. Tell him to return to Santa Fe. Immediately."

Then the sound of the courier's horse's hoofbeats at a gallop, splashing through the rain.

I love my brother; he is my companion, my soulmate, my

twin. I need Juan's smiles to keep away the dark. I need Juan so much, with my father away at the war, and my mother too busy to spend much time with me. I depend on Juan's encouragement to keep trying until I succeeded at a new task, I shelter under Juan's protection from the barbed jibes of our eldest sister. I love Juan like I love my father, with a fierceness that gives my own life meaning.

I have seen wounded soldiers die, and I have seen sick horses die, and I have seen the strongest oxen die of exhaustion as they pulled until they dropped, struggling to clear the trees and boulders to make the new army road through the mountains from Fort Santa Fe to Granada. *If Juan dies, I will die too.*

In our room, my sisters are asleep. I slip silently out from under my blanket and draw my shawl around my head and shoulders, pushing my toes into my Moorish slippers. I go to my mule chest and take out the jeweled portrait of Merina de Cordoba.

I tiptoe from my bedroom down the corridor, past the closed door of my brother's room, to our small royal household chapel. The chapel is lit only by the sacristy lamp, and I kneel before the ivory carving of the Virgin Mary holding the child Jesus. *Please, Holy Mother, do not let my brother die. I will never do anything wrong again. But please, please, do not let Juan die.*

I put my most treasured possession, my father's talisman, at the Virgin's feet as an offering. I look up hopefully. Perhaps the Virgin will answer me, for She is said to speak to the saints, and my good and blameless brother is the best person I know.

I pray for a sign. I bow my head, and somehow, someway, the quiet solace of peace surrounds me. I am helpless, and hopeless. There is nothing I can do. I seem to hear a voice, a tender voice that says, *accept the will of God.*

I creep back to my bed. The bells of the main church of Santa Fe toll three hours past midnight.

✠

Just after sunrise, my father gallops into the fort with Lord Sales at his side. I run to the doorway of our quarters, hiding in the lee of an arch. I see my father and Lord Sales dismount in haste and servants grab the reins of their exhausted, sweat-lathered horses. My mother rushes out to embrace my father.

He holds her passionately. "How is Juan?" Papa can barely bring himself to whisper the words.

"When I sent the messenger, I feared the worst. Doctor Badoc said to summon you." My mother, my strong and queenly mother, weeps like a child in his arms. "At first, I thought Juan had caught a chill, a bad cold. Then it settled in his lungs and he was burned up by fever. I stayed with him, holding his hand, then, just after the bells of three in the morning, the fever broke. Thank God, Juan is breathing normally again, and he now sleeps."

"Thank God and all the saints." Papa makes the sign of the cross. "I feared I would be too late. Don Edmundo rode with me."

Mama closes her eyes. "Our army at Granada?"

"Our troops hold the siege. The officers are waiting my next order."

She nods, and I see Mama leaning against Papa's side. They walk through the archway, to the room of their only son.

I weep with relief, but my pain is like the broken wing of my heart, because my mother and father walk right past me. They do not even see me, standing next to the archway, waiting and listening.

But Lord Sales sees me. Don Edmundo kneels down in front of me, stretching out his hands to my shoulders. I stand frozen, my arms by my side. I feel him patting me awkwardly on the back with his English reserve, and then, as if a barrier breaks, he hugs me tightly to him and I cling to him in return. Neither of us say a word.

From this day forward, I know that Lord Sales will be my greatest protector. Holding me, Lord Edmund Sales finds something he thought lost and buried five years ago in an English churchyard: a father's love for the young daughter that death had taken from him.

"Do you remember the fire last year, Juana?" Lord Sales asks me. He stands up, but keeps his hand on my shoulder.

I lifted my face to him and try to smile as I nod, yes.

"You were a very brave girl then."

"Was I?"

"I thought you were the bravest girl in the world. Even braver than your mother."

When Lord Edmund Sales first came to Santa Fe, our sprawling army camp didn't have a name. It was a rough, raw collection of army tents and lean-to thatched huts, huddled in the middle of the wilderness. Then, last summer, a great fire blazed through, destroying the entire camp.

Lord Sales and I stood near this very spot the morning after the fire, surveying the smoking rubble. We watched my mother calmly assess the devastation. When the queen's advisors, and even my father, said they should give up and return to the Christian army winter headquarters in Seville, my mother said no.

Father Cisneros had made a suggestion. "Perhaps the children should be sent back to Seville?"

"No."

Instead my mother ordered that the camp be rebuilt, not as a ramshackle patchwork of army tents, but this time rising as a solid crusader fortress of stone and brick. She ordered the walls to be whitewashed, brilliant white in the sunshine, so that the Moors could see it from miles away. To her, there is no setback so great that it cannot be overcome. The fort was christened Santa Fe, Holy Faith, the affirmation that the Christian army would never retreat.

I also remembered that in the wake of the fire came the first rumours, the rumours about the Jews.

"Don Edmundo, do you think the Jews started the fire that destroyed our old camp?" I ask.

"No. There is always someone blaming all the bad luck on the Jews. I don't believe it."

"Neither do I. But I've heard gossip."

"Don't let it trouble you." His hand brushes my hair. I feel guilty, for I lost the red silk ribbon he gave me for my birthday. "Are you feeling better now?" he asks.

I nod, yes.

"Good. Best go see how your brother is. I'll come by to see him later."

I slip through the doorway, and Lord Sales strides down the narrow muddy lane to his own quarters.

✠

I long to talk to my brother, but Mama stands in front of the door to his room.

"Can I see Juan, please?"

"He isn't well enough for visitors."

"Visitors! Mama, I'm his sister!"

My mother snaps at me, "The best thing you can do for him is pray for his recovery."

I stagger as if she has slapped me across the face. "Where is Papa?" I ask.

"He's busy with Don Isaac Abravanel. Don't bother him." She stamps her foot in exasperation. "Why can't you be more like your sisters and obey me?"

I look at her with the eyes of my great-grandmother, Merina de Cordoba. She can see that I am not like my sisters. Her words crush me. The comfort of Don Edmundo's kindness fades; I feel lost and hurt. I run into the narrow street outside our quarters.

Where can I go? I pause and remember someone who always listens to me when I am troubled. Doña Beatiz always smiles when she sees me, always has time to talk to me. Doña Beatriz is my mother's best friend, chief lady-in-waiting, and *duenna* to us, the royal daughters. I affectionately call her Tia Beatriz, Auntie Beatriz. She has two grown sons, but no daughter of her own, and she has adopted me as her special favourite. She is never preoccupied with more important things when I need to talk, and she never criticises my needlework, but praises my riding and dancing.

The rain starts again; I pull my cloak over my head and

make my way to Doña Beatriz's house, down the winding narrow streets of Santa Fe. Under my boots, last week's dust is now churned into mud.

The facade of Doña Beatriz's whitewashed house looks like the other buildings – except for the coat-of-arms of her title, 'Condesa de Moya', carved next to the heavy wooden door that faces the street. Once admitted through that outer door, guests enter the flower-filled private patio, then another interior door opens to a cosy world of incomparable grace and elegance. Doña Beatriz de Bobadilla, Condesa de Moya, has the eye of an artist; she has decorated her simple rooms with bright fabrics and pottery vases of perfumed flowers, thick carpets and the softest cushions to sit upon.

She has been part of our wandering army life ever since I can remember. When the Granada War began, Doña Beatriz's husband, Don Sebastian de Leyva, a Knight of Santiago, was appointed *capitan* of troops. During the fight through the mountains above Malaga, Don Sebastian was reported missing in action. His scouting patrol had been ambushed and nothing was ever found of the men.

To this day, the *condesa* doesn't know if her husband Don Sebastian is dead or alive. She remains in the twilight limbo of a widow who is not a widow, waiting until Granada falls, waiting for news of her husband's fate.

I scarcely knew Don Sebastian, but I do know another man who adores the *condesa*: Lord Edmund Sales. Sometimes I tease Don Edmundo about having a secret love – his blundering denials, as he blushes scarlet, are unconvincing protestations. Only Doña Beatriz seems oblivious to his devotion.

The thought of matchmaking makes feel happier: my two favourite grown-ups – Don Edmundo and Doña Beatriz – seem well suited, although I suppose it is disloyal to the distant memory of Don Sebastian de Leyva. I run through the rain to Doña Beatriz's house, past a small group of Moorish camp workers, prisoners-of-war, gathered under a makeshift reed shelter. They are feeding twigs into a crackling, smokey fire to keep off the morning's chill, waiting to be assigned to their tasks for the day.

✠

One of the group, a tall, thin, old man in a black robe and turban, excuses himself to the others, saying he needs to answer a call of nature. He follows Juana down the narrow alley.

He watches a guard open a heavy wooden door in the whitewashed wall and sees the girl enter the house behind it. The old man studies the elaborately carved coat-of-arms next to the door, a sign that someone of great importance lives within. When the guard scowls at him, he bows and touches his turban to leave. He turns the corner quickly to avoid a burly armed warrior, splashing through the mud. It is Lord Edmund Sales.

No matter what his errand in Santa Fe, Lord Sales always takes this route past the house of Doña Beatriz. Lord Sales pauses to chat with the *condesa's* guard briefly, then he continues on his way, whistling cheerfully.

✠

In Doña Beatriz inner courtyard, I shed my wet cloak and call a greeting as I enter her chamber. Standing in the middle of the room is her maid, arms overflowing with a billowing, silk, sapphire-blue gown that she holds for her mistress. Doña Beatriz, dressed in the white linen undershift that she will wear beneath the gown, leans down to kiss me when I rush to embrace her. She smells so lovely, of roses and cinnamon.

Even at what I think of as her advanced age (she is thirty-seven), her skin is smooth as marble, and the bones of her face create a flawless, pleasing structure. Her eyes are coloured a true deep violet, like amethysts, and sparkle with joy and intelligence. She is an extraordinarily beautiful woman. Her long thick hair is a shining curtain of black silk threaded with silver, which falls to her waist. Her figure is slim, with curves in all the right places.

"Juana, my poor dear, what's the matter? Is it your brother? I heard he was better."

"Mama won't let me see him," I sob.

Doña Beatriz holds my face in both her beautiful hands, staring deep into my eyes. "I know how upset you must be, my precious, but we must have faith in God. God will always protect Juan."

Doña Beatriz knows the Granada Prophecy in which my mother firmly believes. "Remember Don Juan's destiny: *a Spanish king to lead us to become the greatest nation in the world, to claim lands yet unknown for God and Spain.*"

Her words are a mixed blessing. Yes, I believe in my brother's destiny, which makes me grieve that my actions caused him harm.

I try to smile, then I step back to greet the *condesa's* maid, Rita. I stroke the silk of the gown she holds, the sapphire-blue gleaming under my fingertips.

"What a beautiful dress! Are you going to wear this to the soldiers' hospital?" I ask the *condesa*.

"No, my dear." Doña Beatriz runs her hands through the ebony curtain of her unbound hair. "No work at the hospital today. Have you heard about the English ambassador?"

I shake my head, no.

"King Henry Tudor is sending a new ambassador from England. We expected him in Spain for Christmas, but his ship caught the fastest winds and he's here now! Your mother says she wants a formal reception for him today. King Henry's envoy must be welcomed properly."

"Mama didn't have time to see the Habsburg Emperor's ambassador." I make a face like I've bitten into a raw olive plucked from the tree. "He's called Father Adrian Boyens. Father Cisneros introduced him to me and my sisters."

"What a presumptive thing for Father Cisneros to do, introducing him to you girls! No, I didn't meet him, but I did see him creeping around the fort. He's gone back north, I believe." She lifts her arms so the maid can slide the heavy gown over her head.

"I hope Father Adrian never, ever, comes back," I say fervently. "The only foreigners I like are the English. Especially Don Edmundo," I pause. "You like Don Edmundo, too, don't you?"

"Mmmm… of course… yes, he's very nice." The *condesa* smooths the front of her gown and the maid ties the sides with ribbon. Rita hands her mistress her jewel box; Doña Beatriz selects a double rope of pearls, with a pendant gold medallion of San Walabonso.

"Are you ready, my darling?" A man's voice comes from the courtyard. Without a pause, Don Alvaro de Braganza enters the room, leaving the courtyard door open behind him. I'm astonished at his easy familiarity in this house.

Don Alvaro is a Portuguese nobleman, and he wears his finest clothes to attend the ambassador's reception. His jacket is of thick, red silk, interwoven with golden thread. Such clothes cost a fortune, but the Portuguese are a wealthy people, far richer than we Spanish. The Portuguese kingdom trades with Africa for gold and ivory, and they grow sugar on their islands of Madiera and the Azores.

While most Portuguese are busy with their sailing routes from Lisbon to these far-off rich lands, a few – like Don Alvaro de Braganza – have volunteered to help us Spanish fight the Moors. He is a commander of the Portuguese Cavalry Regiment, the best horsemen in the world, with the finest and fleetest horses in Christendom.

The fort gossips say that Don Alvaro is Doña Beatriz's lover. I don't believe it; if my Tia Beatriz loves any man other than her missing husband, that man must be Lord Edmund Sales. I look thoughtfully from Doña Beatriz to Don Alvaro. *It's true that Don Alvaro's wife isn't here with him, she stayed in Lisbon. And he is certainly taking liberties, coming in here unannounced.*

Don Alvaro is a magnificent man: tall, with rippling muscles under his fine clothes; dark, curling brown hair and dark brown eyes. He bends down to kiss me in greeting.

Doña Beatriz raises an eyebrow and puts a finger to her lips, signaling him to be discreet.

"Juana, would you please hold this until Rita finishes my hair?" She gives me her rosary and her fan.

The ladies of the court carry these during formal receptions. The men will have their swords, the women their rosaries.

*The power of steel, and the power of prayer.* Doña Beatriz's rosary beads are carved from fragrant rosewood, brought from the Holy Land itself, the beads connected by golden links. Her fan smells of cloves and frankincense, with long, silk, red and blue ribbons attached. A woman can talk without words by the way she handles her fan. I toy with the ribbons, lacing them through my fingers, snapping the fan open and shut like castanets.

Doña Beatriz is seated on a camp stool, her back straight as Rita brushes and arranges her hair. She twists it into an elaborate knot at the back of her head and fixes it with a large, carved, tortoiseshell comb. Doña Beatriz flounces the billowing folds of her silk skirt. She looks like she is seated on a throne instead of a footstool.

The maid finishes and steps back. My eyes widen with admiration. "You look beautiful."

"Indeed she does," Don Alvaro agrees, rather too enthusiastically to suit me.

I step closer to Doña Beatriz, to return her rosary and fan. Then a man's scream stops me. The *condesa's* guard stumbles across the open threshold and falls, wounded, both hands clutching his belly.

Just behind him, a man in a black robe and turban charges into the room. In his upraised hand is a dagger, red with blood.

I can't move as he lunges toward us, but Doña Beatriz rises

swiftly from the footstool and pushes me behind her. The attacker, with a quick sideways slash of the blade, cuts across her beautiful face. He then thrusts the dagger across her breast toward her heart.

Don Alvaro jumps forward with drawn sword, but the assailant whirls and chops his blade across the nobleman's right wrist. Don Alvaro's sword falls and the attacker lunges with a stabbing thrust.

He shouts in Arabic, "Death to the infidels! Death to you, King Fernando and Queen Isabel!"

I drop the rosary and fan and back away, hand to my mouth, stepping into the blood that pools near Doña Beatriz's body. I look up at the assailant's face.

I realise that I know him: it is the *jihadi* from the Moors' cave.

The maid Rita screams for help and throws herself across the body of her mistress. I stumble to the door, nearly colliding with an armed man, who charges into the room, sword drawn.

It is Lord Edmund Sales. He roars a challenge in English and the assassin turns from Don Alvaro to face him, dagger poised. Lord Sales takes a feint back, then, with a cutting blow from his sword, chops the knife from the assassin's right hand. The fingers are severed, falling with the knife to the floor. Howling with fury, the assassin leaps at Lord Sales and, with the bleeding stumps of his fingers, claws at the Englishman's eyes.

Lord Sales uses the flat of his sword to knock the *jihadi* on the side of the head, stunning him and driving him to his knees. Two men-at-arms run in, alerted by the maid's screams and cries of "Assassins!"

"Hold him, just hold him! Don't kill him," Lord Sales

shouts in English, reverting to his own language in the chaos. The guards hesitate, not understanding his words. Somehow I find my voice and translate his orders.

The two men-at-arms grab the attacker and push him face-down on the floor. Lord Sales turns to the *condesa*, lying silently, her maid kneeling next to her body.

Doña Beatriz's sapphire-blue dress is soaked with large, dark patches of blood. Lord Sales lifts her head, which lolls against his arm, the skin of her face torn from the forehead to the jaw, the bones white underneath. A trickle of blood runs from her mouth and nose; her left eye is a bloody jelly. He touches the side of her neck, feeling for the artery and the faint pulse of life.

The devoted Rita mutely offers help. Lord Sales sees me standing in front of him, shivering with fear.

"Take care of Doña Beatriz," he says to the maid. His eyes sweep the room for other possible assassins, but he finds no more. He sheaths his sword and picks me up.

I sense, somehow, that as much as he loves the *condesa*, Lord Sales is determined to keep me safe.

I hold on to Don Edmundo. I am drifting in and out of consciousness when Lord Sales reaches my father.

I hear my father's voice: "Oh God, no, my little girl… is she…"

"She's safe, Don Fernando, Juana is safe." Lord Sales says, handing me into my father's arms.

My father cradles me to his chest. I open my eyes and Papa kisses me. He hugs me fiercely and puts me back on my feet so he can draw his sword. I lean against him, feeling the anger coursing through him.

"In the name of all the saints, what is happening?" he demands.

"A *jihadi* assassin just tried to kill Doña Beatriz and Don Alvaro," Lord Sales says. "Your daughter was in the *condesa's* house. I was in the street close by, when I heard the *condesa's* guard being attacked. I ran to help."

"I don't understand. Why would a *jihadi* assassin want to kill Doña Beatriz and Don Alvaro?"

"Don Alvaro and Doña Beatriz were dressed for the ambassador's reception, wearing their richest clothes and jewels. When the assassin found them, he mistook them for a king and queen. The assassin's target was you and Queen Isabel, but he got it wrong."

My father's face went white. "Bring him to me."

The men-at-arms drag the assassin to King Fernando. His black turban has been knocked off and the pink scalp is peppered with wet, wispy, grey hairs. They toss him on the ground before my father and one of the soldiers stamps his boot in the small of the old man's back to pin him down.

I have never seen my father so angry. He stares at the *jihadi* and asks Lord Sales, "Doña Beatriz and Don Alvaro…are they…?"

"They're wounded – badly – but alive when I left them."

"Send Doctor Badoc immediately." A crowd is gathering, and servants from the royal household push closer to see what is happening.

My father turns to the captain of the guard. "Did this man say anything?" he says, gesturing with his sword.

"He shouted – in Arabic – that he killed the king and queen. And that he rejoices in their deaths."

Queen Isabel comes out of the house and goes to her husband's side. Within the security of Fort Santa Fe, my mother never has bodyguards with her. Neither do we children.

"*Jihadis* show us no mercy," my father says, his voice shivering with rage, his sword still pointed at the prisoner on the ground in front of him. "King Boabdil of Granada says he wants peace. I ask him for a truce, and this – this! – is the messenger he sends us?"

I want to cry out, *No! I heard King Boabdil argue with this man. This assassin must have followed me here on his own.* But no words come aloud.

Papa thrusts his sword back into its scabbard, and grabs my hand in his own, holding it firm.

Mama says, "Doctor Badoc is on his way to the *condesa's* house." She puts a restraining hand on my father's arm. "We must not let anything the enemy does frighten us."

"Frighten us? They just tried to kill us both."

"But we have been spared, and we must not hide ourselves away. I will hold the reception for the the English ambassador, as planned," my mother says.

My father nods in grim agreement, then turns to Lord Sales and the men-at-arms. "First, I will return King Boabdil's messenger."

I watch as soldiers drag the old man, barely conscious, through the hostile crowd that yells and jostles after them to the edge of the fort. The place buzzes with anger, like a hornet's nest hammered with a stick. My mother returns into the family quarters, to quiet my sisters, reassure my sick brother and prepare for the English ambassador.

I go with Papa, the crowd giving way before us, to the place where the animals are slaughtered. My father never lets go of my hand, holding with a grip so tight that it brings tears to my eyes.

The master-butcher Paco is at his stand, and the guards throw their prisoner into the rough wooden trestle where the pig carcasses are cut up. The assassin opens his blackened eyes and whimpers when he smells the unmistakable stench of pig.

Papa leans down to explain to me, "To the *jihadi*, the pig is unclean. To die here on the pigs' scaffold, with the remains of the beast, will condemn him to hell."

I long to run away, but I press closer to my father, who stands upright and impassive. And I watch.

Two of the soldiers hold the struggling man down, and the butcher expertly slices his large, heavy knife across the man's throat, almost cutting off the head. The *jihadi's* scream trails off into a gurgle, with bubbles of bright pink air frothing from his severed windpipe.

Then the knife expertly carves between the vertebrae, and the head falls away.

Papa's face is without emotion as he watches, and I hug close to his side. Lord Sales stands next to me, his eyes searching the crowd for any suspicious strangers.

The butcher rolls the body over and chops off both hands, then breaks through the joints of the the arms and the legs. He turns the body again, and changes to a different sharp knife to disembowel it. He continues to chop the flesh into smaller pieces and tosses them into a basket by his stand. The blood runs through the basket's woven sides onto the muddy ground.

The crowd seethes with menace and the air hums with a palpable sense of retribution, of harsh justice.

I tug at Papa's hand. He looks down, as if realising for the first time that I am with him. Lord Sales gently touches my shoulder.

"May I take Juana back to her mother?" he asks my father.

"Yes, of course."

The crowd parts for us. When I return home, my mother puts me to bed. I sip a warm drink prepared for me by Doctor Badoc, before I fall into a dreamless and troubled sleep.

✠

My father orders his men to take the basket, with the assassin's butchered remains, to the army's front line at Granada. There, using the great catapult that fires missiles up and over the city walls, soldiers hurl the bloody fragments through the air, and they fall to earth in the cloistered gardens of the Alhambra.

The foreign *jihadis* in Granada collect the pieces of Muktada Bin Kadim's body and sew it together with black silk thread. They give him a martyr's burial.

✠

While I sleep and my brother remains in bed next door, Mama organises the reception for the English ambassador, Lord Thomas Lisle. My father joins her, with my three sisters in attendance.

When the reception ends and my sisters return to our bedroom, little Catalina wakes me with her news. She is dancing with happiness. "Oh Juana, I'm engaged! I'm going to marry the Prince of Wales!"

"What?" I rise to one elbow, drowsy still from the sleeping potion. "But you're only six years old!"

My eldest sister Isabella looks smug as she fluffs up her pillow. "That makes no difference," she says tartly. "The English ambassador came with a a special request. King Henry Tudor of England wants a bride for his son. Prince Arthur is five years old, so Mama said Catalina would be perfect for him."

Catalina continues dancing around the room, humming happily, just out of reach of the servant trying to catch her to remove her court dress. "I'm going to stay here with all of you until I'm older, but I'll be called 'The Princess of Wales' right away. Isn't it wonderful?"

Isabella smiles at Catalina's antics and catches her hands as she dances by. "Let's get ready for bed, Princess," she says. "Now we are both brides-to-be. I've accepted the King of Portugal, and one day your Prince Arthur will be King of England. We will be sister queens!" The two of them fuss happily, as the new Princess of Wales is slipped into her nightgown. The maids clap their hands with pride and delight.

My eight-year-old sister Maria silently comes over to sit on my bed, cuddling her little pet dog in her arms. "That leaves just you and me," she says sadly. "Oh Juana, I do so much want to get married one day and have lots of babies." Her little dog, Chica, snuggles closer to her.

I reach out and fondle Chica's ears. I say nothing, but I wonder if I will ever marry anyone.

"What about us, Juana?" Maria asks plaintively. "Who will marry us? Will we ever become queens, too?"

*Perhaps, that night, it was a blessing that I could not see into the future. For it is my sister Maria and I who will one day wear the greater crowns, and the weight of my own will almost crush me.*

✠

The next day King Boabdil prepares an elaborate parchment scroll, covered in intricate calligraphy in both Arabic and Spanish, heavy with great green and gold seals and ribbons, to send to King Fernando and Queen Isabel. It is a request for an armistice – a stop to the fighting – to begin peace talks to end the Granada War.

Father Cisneros says a Mass of thanksgiving for the armistice, for Juan's recovery and to celebrate Catalina and Prince Arthur's engagement. Royal couriers ride to Seville and Barcelona with the news, and a ship is dispatched to London with gifts and messages for King Henry Tudor and the young Prince of Wales.

But for my parents, the war remains paramount. My mother announces that she will now move our family from Fort Santa Fe to my father's army camp, near the walls of Granada.

"While the peace talks continue," she says briskly, "we will camp in full view of King Boabdil and wait for his surrender."

The servants pack the mule trains with our tents and supplies. This is the life I have always known, the familiar nomadic routine, on the move from one army camp to the next.

I am packing my personal chest when my brother Juan

confronts me. His recovery has been as rapid as the illness that struck him down, and his renewed health is considered a sign of divine favour.

He holds out his hand, palm up. There is the portrait of Merina de Cordoba. "I found this on the chapel altar, near the statue of the Virgin," he says.

"I put it there, as a promise and a gift, to the Virgin. For saving your life." I leave unspoken, *And for saving mine. God knows, I cannot live without you.*

"Well, my life is back." He gently curls my fingers around the talisman. I feel the cool strength of his hand enclosing mine. "This jewel is yours, Juana. You must keep it with you, all the way to Granada."

I kiss my brother on the cheek and secure the talisman in my bodice.

When we leave, Santa Fe is garrisoned with just a few soldiers. The hospital stays open for the wounded, with the doctors and nursing nuns on duty.

Doña Beatriz remains in her Santa Fe home to recover. Doctor Badoc saved the *condesa's* life, but he could not salvage her beauty. To close the ragged knife wound across her face, he made tiny, delicate stitches with silk thread, but the scars will remain. Her left eye is gone, with an empty socket. When she recovered consciousness, Doña Beatriz refused to admit anyone but my mother into her sickroom; she did not want me or my sisters to see her. The faithful Don Edmundo was turned away from her door by her maid; he handed Rita flowers to give to her mistress. He had picked a bouquet of mountain rosemary, its tiny blue flowers carrying the message of remembered love. Doña Beatriz lay still, in her darkened room, stroking the fragrant, slim, green branches with her fingertips.

Don Alvaro de Braganza convalesced slowly from his wounds, with his wife hurrying from Lisbon to nurse him back to health.

✠

I am weary with hours of riding, then, ahead of us, I see my first glimpse of the towering walls of Granada. I straighten up in the saddle, reining Tinto to a halt. My sisters and brother stop their horses also. The Alhambra Palace, on its hill in the distance – perhaps only three miles aways from where our tent is pitched – is breathtakingly beautiful, shining red-gold in the sunset. The Moorish name, *Al-hambra*, means 'the red' fortress.

Juan and I look at each other, and I know he feels as I do. *This is our destiny; every sign and portent has led us here.*

The wind blows towards us from Granada. On the breeze, I hear the *muezzin*, chanted by the *imams* high in the minarets of Granada's mosques, calling the Muslim faithful to prayer. The haunting sound trails through the air like an unfurling melodic banner. I think of King Boabdil, praying behind the walls.

Life will change when Granada is ruled by Christians. Muslims in Spanish Christian cities are not allowed the loud public call to prayer from their minarets; in a compromise edict, the *muezzin* can only be chanted softly in the interiors of mosques themselves, like celestial whispers. It was a similar law for Christians in Spanish Muslim cities: no public pealing of church bells, only small bells could be used discreetly inside the church building.

I feel someone watching me. I turn to see Lord Sales, as he pauses to listen to the *muezzin*.

Once Lord Edmund Sales' English archers and my parents' army take the city, the minarets of Granada will be silenced forever.

✠

In our army camp, the great Silver Cross dominates the most prominent position, facing the Alhambra. Adjacent to the Silver Cross is a tented chapel, and next to that, our family tent.

I sag in the saddle with relief. *Here at last!* Then, I stare with horror at an apparition from my darkest nightmare. Father Adrian Boyens peers past the guards and bows to welcome us.

"What is he doing here?" I turn to Juan.

My brother shrugs and dismounts from his horse. "Father Cisneros told me that Father Adrian was in Seville when the armistice was announced, so he decided to come here rather than return to Austria."

Juan gives Father Adrian a polite salute. I refuse to look at the priest. I slide out of the saddle, give Tinto's reins to a servant, and stamp angrily into our tent.

✠

At midnight, in a part of the army camp far away from the royal tent, Father Adrian Boyens, ambassador of Emperor

Maximilian Habsburg of Austria and special envoy of Flanders and the Duchy of Burgundy, tosses restlessly in his bed and stares up into the darkness. There is a glimmer of starlight where the tentpole punches through the sagging canvas.

Father Adrian thinks to himself, *I hate sharing this tent with the English ambassador,* as Sir Thomas Lisle snores loudly from the nearby bed. His mood sours. Not enough tents to go around, so ambassadors and petitioners have to double-up and share. *Tents! Even the Spanish royals are living in a tent. The Trastamara family has no sense of comfort. Camping out, cooking over open fires like mountain shepherds. Dear God in heaven, can you see the Habsburg family in this wilderness? It beggars belief.*

Father Adrian tosses on his hard pallet. *The English ambassador Sir Thomas is insufferable. Crowing about his diplomatic triumph: the youngest daughter – little Catalina – is now engaged to King Henry Tudor's son.* He feels his stomach churning, and the taste of garlic and olive oil bubbles up in his throat. *God's teeth, how I hate Spanish food.*

He shivers and pulls his fur robe up to his chin. The November nights are cool here, but Father Adrian prefers the Andalucian winter cold to Spain's scorching summer heat. *The Andalucians complain about the cold? They should be in Austria or Flanders in the winter, when the rivers and lakes freeze solid and the earth is so iron-hard you cannot bury the dead. Any little Spanish princess coming North is in for a rude awakening. Even that hot-tempered Juana.*

Father Adrian listens to the rain starting again, beating against the canvas roof of the tent. *The rainwater will probably start pouring through that hole above me, and I'll get soaked. How did Sir Thomas Lisle get the better bed?* He sighs. *At least this afternoon I got a formal introduction to Queen Isabel and King Fernando.*

They reluctantly agreed to see Father Adrian Boyens after he waved a letter from Seville under their noses, from the Grand Inquisitor Torquemada, with a demand for an audience.

While he was in Seville, Father Adrian formed a bond with the grand inquisitor, from the first moment he was ushered into the Inquisition headquarters, Castillo San Jorge, on the banks of the Guadalquiver river. *Grand Inquisitor Torquemada is a man after my own heart,* he thought.

Father Adrian was pleased at how eagerly the inquisitor listened to his ideas on crushing heretics, *conversos* and Jews. "After all, Grand Inquisitor," Father Adrian had told him, "in the Northern countries of Christian Europe we have outlawed Jews for centuries. No Jewish problem in Austria, Flanders, Burgundy or England. You have them all here in Spain!" He allowed himself a smile of pride. "I, Adrian Boyens, can teach you Spanish how to run an Inquisition. I can solve your Jewish problem in no time."

Across the tent, the sleeping English ambassador utters a series of snorting snores, like a badly-beaten drum. Father Adrian opens his eyes wide, then squeezes them shut. *I'll never get to sleep if that English jackass keeps up this racket. If he doesn't stop snoring, I swear that I will suffocate him with his own pillow.*

Suddenly, the bed creaks alarmingly as the Englishman shifts his position. The snoring stops, and the ensuing silence is filled with quiet breathing. *Thank God for that!* Father Adrian thinks.

After his fruitful meeting with Grand Inquisitor Torquemada, Father Adrian sees a whole new world opening for him in Spain with a powerful ally. *I'll not waste my time befriending that old fool Father Cisneros. He may be the royal family's chaplain, but he has no 'cojones', as the Spanish say. Cisneros thinks that I'm looking for a wife for my widowed master, Maxmilian Habsburg. But I'm playing a longer game: the next generation. I need a man to whom the future belongs.*

Father Adrian Boyens is a man of limitless ambition. He was born of a humble family in Flanders and began his upward trajectory by joining the church, then hitching his star to the Heiress of Flanders – the Duchess Mary of Burgundy. He became her prime advisor and confidant. *Poor Mary, he thinks. Died so young, poor woman, just a few years after her wedding to Maximilian Habsburg. What a pity about that 'hunting accident'. Which left motherless her two children, a little five-year-old boy and a three-year-old girl.*

Father Adrian Boyens arranged to be appointed guardian of Mary's children. The Habsburgs are not a close-knit family, like the Trastamaras. Their father, Emperor Maximilian Habsburg, remains in Austria, with his children a thousand miles away – being raised in the decadent, elegant court of Burgundy and Flanders.

Phillipe Habsburg is now almost fourteen years old, nicknamed Phillipe the Fair, for his good looks. He is athletic, indolent and sensuous. Father Adrian thinks, *my young Duke of Burgundy is happy to give me the boring tasks of state, so he can hunt, drink and chase girls. His sister, the young Duchess Margaret, now twelve, is a spoiled, willful little shrew. But I know how to handle her, too.*

*I must look to the future of my young charges. If the Trastamaras defeat the Moors – which I didn't think possible at first – if they win*

*Granada, I've got to be on the winning side. The Trastamaras have spent the war teetering on the edge of bankruptcy, but winning Granada – and its gold – will make them the richest royal family in Christendom. The Spanish royals live in a nest of Jews, but the Inquisition can change that. The sooner, the better.*

*If I can arrange a rich marriage for young Phillipe, I will be set forever. My Habsburgs have grand titles and land, but they are poor and always in debt. With my Habsburg backing and the Trastamara fortune, I can aim higher than any mere priest or ambassador.*

As he drifted off to sleep, Father Adrian Boyens saw himself in Flanders, in the cathedral at Lille, having a bishop's mitre placed on his head. Then he saw himself in Spain, in the Cathedral of Toledo, ceremoniously donning a cardinal's scarlet brimmed hat. And then, then in a great convocation at St. Peter's Basilica in Rome, he saw himself crowned with the massive papal tiara. *Pope Adrian…*

✠

After midnight, the rain stops and the temperature drops to near-freezing. In the Jewish quarter of the tented camp, Doña Sara Abravenel grumbles as she tucks a fur robe over her husband's lap. The royal treasurer sits at his wooden desk – in reality just a folding table with a horn lantern on top of it – his feet in fur-lined boots next to a *brasero* with glowing charcoal. His breath makes little puffs of white in the air. His hands are cold, even inside his thick, silk gloves.

"I'm going to bed," Sara says, as she tenderly kisses his cheek. "It's too cold to stay up." She looks over his shoulder at the columns of figures, with an expert eye. His accounts, the lines of numbers added up, crossed out, added up again.

"Not good?" she asks.

Don Isaac takes off his spectacles and taps the frame on the top page.

"There is, maybe, just enough gold to keep the Christian army going for two more weeks. After that, who knows?"

"Boabdil will surely surrender before then. How much longer can they talk? No supplies can get in. The Moors have gold, but you can't cook gold to eat."

Don Isaac nods. His wife is the practical one. He moves the lantern closer and reaches for a freshly-cut quill. The tips of his silk gloves are stained with ink.

"Each day the Moors make a new request, then the Christians counter that with a new demand. Nobody wants the fighting to start again, so they talk, talk, talk. The royal treasury is running out of money." Don Isaac puts his spectacles back on.

"Will you be long?" Sara asks. "Should I bring you some soup?"

He pats his wife's forearm. "No, thank you. Go to sleep, my dear. I'll join you soon."

Sara hesitates. "There has been news from Seville. My sister's son, Gregorio."

Don Isaac closes his eyes and sighs. His wife's nephew, the *converso*. A bright twenty-five-year-old, who became a Christian. He remembered gathering with the other elders of the synagogue to sit *shiva* for him, when the young man announced his conversion three years ago. To the strictly observant Jewish community, Gregorio – his Christian baptismal name – is considered dead. With his immediate family, there is still clandestine contact.

Sara's voice trembles. "The Inquisition took him for questioning, with other *conversos* from the neighborhood. My sister has heard nothing since. She thought perhaps with your contacts, you might be able to…"

"I will try to talk to the queen."

"I'm so worried, Isaac. Inquisitor Torquemada puts *conversos* through 'trials of faith'. *Auto de fe*. Some have been burned at the stake. My sister is terrified for her son, and afraid for all of us. She says that the Inquisition won't stop with the *conversos*, but will come for everyone in the Jewish community."

Isaac clasps his wife's trembling hand. "No, that's impossible under the laws of Spain. The Inquisition is limited by law to hunting *conversos*. Our own Jewish community is protected by the Christian monarchs. King Fernando personally promises us his protection, and he keeps his promises. For the future, the heir, Don Juan, is a good young man who will continue that protection. Rest easy, my dear. I will do what I can about Gregorio."

Sara squeezes his hand in return, and kisses him goodnight.

Don Isaac stares blankly at his papers. *All this worry with the war and now the Inquisition, too. Sara and I are getting old, too old to be spending winter in a campaign tent.* He lays his quill down, and wishes they were back in their comfortable home in Seville.

They live in the Jewish Quarter, adjacent to the royal palace of the Alcazar. *Our house was built by the Moors, of course, like nearly everything in that city. Arab architects create the most beautiful buildings in the world.* The great Moorish Andalucian cities of Granada, Seville and Cordoba echo their majestic counterparts in the East: Damascus, Baghdad. And Jerusalem.

*Ah, Jerusalem.* Sacred to all three faiths, now conquered and claimed by the Muslims, and coveted by the Christians. The city that Don Isaac's ancestors had been forced to abandon in the days of the Roman Empire, when they migrated to the safety of Spain. *And here we have settled, known as the Sephardim. But should I return to Jerusalem?*

Don Isaac knows that Spanish Christians believe a cataclysmic event will shatter the world by the year 1500. They talk of the Granada Prophecy, which foretells of a Spanish king who will take the cross to new worlds, and even – God willing – one day claim Jerusalem. *Well, if the Spanish army is going as far as Jerusalem, I want to be there.*

Don Isaac waits until he hears Sara settling into bed, and the familiar, rhythmic, light breathing of her sleep. Then he slides the hidden letter out from under the accounts. He cuts the seal, unfolds the paper page and holds it with both hands, closer to the lamp.

The letter was brought to him earlier, by private courier, from Cordoba. It is in Hebrew script, without names or salutations, but Don Isaac knows the writing: Don Simon Benavente, curator of the medical library at Cordoba.

As you know, many overseas scholars come to study our texts in Cordoba, but we have had a recent visitor about whom I feel the greatest unease. He is a Christian priest from the North and he stopped here after visiting Seville.

He spent several days researching our medical library. On his last day, he tried to to smuggle out a restricted document, concealed in his robe, but my assistants are very vigilant and caught him. He claimed it was an oversight. He gave the document back, but with very bad grace.

It was a medical treatise, which, because of the nature of the knowledge therein, is kept in a locked chest. He had been given authorisation and a key to the chest by Grand Inquisitor Torquemada of Seville. The foreigner's name is Adrian Boyens.

I send you this warning because the document is the only one of its kind, dating from ancient antiquity. It details the use of the rarest poisons, which can kill and leave no trace. It also identifies the only known antidotes, which are even more rare than the poisons themselves.

Don Isaac stares at the letter. He carefully tears the paper into small pieces, which he feeds to the glowing coals of the *brasero*. It hurts his back to lean down awkwardly to do so, but he patiently watches until every last, tiny fragment of the letter has flared and burnt to grey cinders.

✠

The peace negotiations with King Boabdil stall. "Tomorrow, a final agreement," the Moorish envoys say. When tomorrow comes, King Boabdil asks for one more day in his beloved city.

"Perhaps we should go back to Santa Fe and negotiate with him from there?" one of the queen's courtiers suggests tentatively. "It would be more comfortable." The winter wind blows coldly from the Sierra Nevada, shaking the tents.

"We will not move, except into Granada." My mother turns her eyes to the courtier with a stare even colder than the wind. She is not in a good mood, for she has just come from a conference with her treasurer, Don Isaac Abravenel.

He had placed a sheet of paper before her, with long columns of figures and ink-stains, corrections and notes in the margins. Don Isaac's face was grave. "My Lady, it is good that the peace talks are continuing, but meanwhile we still have to feed the soldiers. I estimate that we have enough gold to keep the army going for two weeks. And then…" He holds his palm upward and empty.

Each morning, I watch the group of Spanish knights ride under a flag of truce from our army camp to the City of Granada, and each evening, I watch them return. The riders emerge from the silver mist veiling the hill of the Alhambra, shoulders slumped. Again, no final surrender. King Boabdil requests just one more day, just one more concession. Above us, thin skeins of red clouds thread through the darkening sky.

✠

Soon it will be Christmas, and the weather alternates between pouring, icy rain and wind-bitten cold. The weather has no effect on my mother, and my father makes sure that we children and his soldiers have warm cloaks and wood for the campfires.

At supper, we gather inside our tent, wrapped in furs. We sit around a low, circular table, with a hot *brazero* – glowing with coals – underneath it. A large, heavy cloth covers the top of the table, with generously big borders, so the edges can be pulled over our laps. It creates a warm cosy den for our lower legs and feet.

My father sits with me on his left side and Juan on his right. My mother is opposite him, with Maria and our Princess of Wales, Catalina. Our eldest sister, Isabella, says she is not hungry and she doesn't join us. She often refuses to eat and I think it strange, for Isabella is thin as a pitchfork. *She'll be the skinniest Queen of Portugal, ever.*

The leather doorway of the tent is pulled open and Lord Edmund Sales enters, shakes off his heavy woolen cloak and hands it to a servant.

I welcome him with my brightest smile and all the family call out greetings, urging him to join our supper. He seats himself next to me, and I am thrilled. I am between my two favourite men – my father on one side of me and Don Edmundo on the other. I hear his knee joints creak loudly as he lowers himself to sit cross-legged on one of the large pillows that circle the *brazero*. I giggle when I catch Juan's eyes, for we know that Don Edmundo finds the Andalucian seating pillows – *almohadas* – a trial. He prefers chairs.

My mother offers him the main dish of venison stew, which is cooked in wine, garlic and saffron, with a touch of lemon, and served with almonds and rice.

"Any news on the surrender?" he asks.

"Nothing definite from King Boabdil," my mother replies.

"It must be difficult for him," my brother says. "We call him King Boabdil, but among his own people he is called 'sultan'. The Moors believe that only God is king, and they use the word 'sultan' to describe an earthly ruler."

"I don't care what he calls himself, I just want him to surrender," my father says. My mother nods in agreement.

Don Edmundo ladles the stew from the serving dish into his own bowl. He sniffs the steaming aroma appreciatively. "Where did you get the venison?" he asks.

"Juan killed a deer, with the English longbow you taught him to use," I say. "I shot a rabbit with my longbow, and we ate the rabbit yesterday."

"Well done," Don Edmundo beams. "You've got to start young to learn to use the longbow. You two are just the right age. All English archers begin training at your age." Don Edmundo speaks to us in his own unique combination of English, badly accented Spanish and stumbling Latin. Whenever his vocabulary leaves the others confused, I translate, because I always understand him perfectly.

My father nods to a servant to bring Don Edmundo wine. "King Boabdil's stalling is bad enough, but now the *jihadis* are threatening to mine the Alhambra Palace with gunpowder and blow it up before we get there."

I catch my breath sharply.

My mother shakes her head. "They won't do that. Whatever we think of King Boabdil, he loves his city. He won't let anyone destroy the Alhambra."

My father takes another sip of wine and raises his glass to Don Edmundo. "Here's to the Moorish architects. There's an old Spanish saying, 'The Moors build the cities, the Christians build the armies and the Jews pay for it all'."

Don Edmundo smiles, but my mother frowns at his remark. Papa continues. "It's always foreign fanatics who cause problems in Andalucia. Outsiders aren't like us. They break the rules of chivalry by sending an assassin into my home and striking at the heart of my family."

Don Edmundo slowly puts his bowl down and from his eyes I can see that the memory of that day haunts him. He looks at my mother. "How is Doña Beatriz?"

"Recovering, but slowly," my mother says gently. "I spoke with her before we left the fort."

"Thank God she is still alive," he says. My eyes fill with tears. I snuggle next to Don Edmundo on the large *almohada*, and he puts his arm around me. I look up at him. *With Don Alvaro back with his wife in Portugal, Tia Beatriz, when she gets better, will find out how constant and devoted this Englishman is.*

My father gestures to the servant to pour Don Edmundo another glass of wine.

"Perhaps we can celebrate Christmas in the Alhambra?" my sister Maria says hopefully. She is feeding her dog Chica tidbits from her plate.

"Not this year, Maria," my mother says in a resigned voice. "Tomorrow is Christmas Eve."

✠

Our family gathers in the tented chapel adjacent to the Silver Cross. Near the altar is the Christmas crib – with carved tiny figures of the Baby Jesus, Mary and Joseph. There are carved figures of shepherds in Andalucian dress, and three kings who look like Moorish potentates.

We gather around the Christmas crib and sing carols. Juan composes several new songs for the occasion. His face is radiant with the music and he plays his guitar to accompany the *coro*, the carol singers, with flair and passion.

At midnight on Christmas Eve, 1491, we Christians ring the bells. We ring the bells so long and so loud that every Moor in the besieged City of Granada can hear the peals.

We light large bonfires around the Silver Cross, so that it shines brightly against the black velvet night sky. Every Moorish soldier guarding Granada can see it clearly.

*King Boabdil knows that we Christians are waiting on the hill across the valley, waiting on the other side of the high red walls of the Alhambra, waiting for him to give us his city.*

✠

At dawn, I slip out of bed to stand outside the royal tent and listen to the call of the *muezzin* across the valley. It is the first prayer of the day for the Moors, and the second day of January of the year 1492. I have my sister Isabella's fur cape pulled over my shoulders, the thick collar framing my face. Isabella will snap like a civet cat if she finds me with her new cape, a gift from the King of Portugal, but I think it is worth the risk.

I nuzzle the fur around my neck. My breath makes little clouds in the cold air.

I hear a solitary set of hoofbeats approach our tent, where my father is already at work, preparing his papers to brief his knights before they ride once again to Granada to negotiate.

The guard orders the Moorish horseman to halt and demands his sword. He indicates that he has no weapon; he comes as an unarmed courier. My father looks up from his papers, through the open tent flap, and tells the man to approach him.

The Moorish courier bows. His message is short. "Sultan Boabdil is ready to sign your final terms for the surrender of the City of Granada. His personal treasury and the gold reserves of the city will be turned over to you. In return for a peaceful surrender, the sultan accepts your promise that the citizens of Granada will not be harmed; that their homes and businesses will be safe. The mosques of the city will not be violated. We will be allowed to keep our religion."

"Agreed."

The messenger pulls a rolled document, with a heavy seal, from his pouch. He hands it to the king. "Sultan Boabdil wishes your signature and seal. The city is yours."

"What? Now? Sign today?"

"Now."

My father presses the fingertips of his hands over his closed eyelids. He then puts his hands down, palms flat, on the document which he has spread on the table before him. He stares ahead of him as if seeing into another world.

"Send for the queen," he says in voice barely above a whisper. The page standing behind his chair slips out silently.

The courier shifts nervously. "The sultan asks that you make haste. He fears the foreign *jihadis* might yet try to destroy the Alhambra Palace. He has no control over them. He asks that you send an advance guard to secure the city now, then make your own formal entrance into Granada when you are ready."

I gasp at the news and run to tell my brother.

Within the hour, my parents – King of Aragon and Queen

of Castile – give orders to their most trusted commanders. By afternoon, Lord Sales and his English archers march into Granada, alongside the disciplined Spanish knights of the Order of Santiago. There, they replace, as agreed, one-to-one, the Moorish sentries at each of the city gates and watchtowers.

Before the Christian soldiers arrive, the foreign *jihadis* disappear from the city, slipping away, riding to the coast for ships that will take them back from whence they came.

It is decided that on the sixth of January, 1492, the day in the Christian calendar to commemorate the Epiphany, the Trastamara family will ride through the main gate of Granada to accept the keys to the city. *Granada is ours at last.*

✠

On the morning of the 6th of January, 1492, my mother is like a girl in her delight; my father's eyes are bright with excitement. Our family has spent the last few days planning what we will wear for the ceremonial entrance to the city, how we will caparison our horses and the order of the procession.

King Fernando and Queen Isabel ride first, flanked by the bearers with the embroidered silk battle flags of Castile and Aragon. Next is Juan, Prince of the Asturias, heir to the united Spanish throne, riding alongside Father Cisneros, who represents the church. Then, in order of precedence, ride Isabella – engaged to the King of Portugal – and Catalina, now the Princess of Wales. Maria and I are the last, for our two sisters now outrank us with their betrothals.

Then come the officers and knights of the army, followed by the Spanish regiments. Riding at the end of the procession are the foreign ambassadors, including Sir Thomas Lisle, representing England, and Father Adrian Boyens, representing the Habsburg Emperor. The English archers are already in Granada, poised on top of the city walls, to guard us.

My mother warns us to ride proud and tall, and not to panic. "No matter what happens," she says. There is still the danger of a *jihadi* attack. The threat of assassination hangs over us, heightening the tension.

My father orders sentries to line the route into Granada, a distance of three miles, with men-at-arms stationed every hundred yards on both sides of the road. The sentries watch both the silent Moorish crowds and the empty spaces with vigilance.

The morning of the procession is cold and clear; to me the sky seems as blue as the robe of the Blessed Virgin. Heavier snow has fallen on the Sierra Nevada mountains overnight, a white lace *mantilla* draped over rocky shoulders of grey velvet.

On our approach to the city, we ride through a small whitewashed Moorish village. These tiny farming *pueblos* lie at the foot of La Sabika, the hill on which the Alhambra Palace stands. I see the Moorish peasants staring at my unveiled face, and the unveiled faces of my sisters.

Riding through the village, I wince as we trample their vegetable plots under our horses' hooves, scattering the carefully-placed white pebbles that delineate their borders. The Moorish farmers bow their turbaned heads in silent resignation. I see, huddled under the olive trees, the farmers' wives pulling headscarves over their faces, holding their children close to them.

When we reach the cobbled streets of Granada, only

Moorish men and boys are to be seen. The ladies of the city remain cloistered, an invisible presence behind the shutters of enclosed balconies. I hear the occasional sob, the hushed wailing of a baby.

When we ride past a mosque, there is a loud explosion, perhaps gunfire, and my horse Tinto shies, his hooves scrabbling on the paving stones. My brother reins his own horse in, looking back to see if Maria and I are safe, but my parents never pause.

A sound like crashing ocean waves, one following the other, begins behind me. I sit up even taller in my saddle. The sound is the roll of the Spanish army drums, with 150 soldier-drummers beating cadence. I feel the rhythm hammering like a giant's heartbeat, amplified by the stone walls of the city.

Drum. Drum. Drum-drum-drum.

Drum. Drum. Drum-drum-drum.

A slow march. The soldiers in perfect order. The drummers precede the priests who carry the great Silver Cross, holding it high. Behind the Cross, in order of precedence, come the knights of the Orders of Santiago, Calatrava and Alcantara.

Drum. Drum. Drum-drum-drum.

Drum. Drum. Drum-drum-drum.

I see Lord Sales up on the ramparts, with his English bowmen. They are placed as sentries on top of the walls, ready to unleash a firestorm of arrows on anyone daring to break the peace among the Moorish citizens and refugees lining the streets.

Drum. Drum. Drum-drum-drum.
Drum. Drum. Drum-drum-drum.

The parade file of soldiers, boots marching over the cobblestones, stretches for nearly a mile, following the Silver Cross.

The wind picks up, even colder now, and the sky turns from ice blue to grey, and flurries of snow blow around my face. I look down at the snowflakes melting on my new riding gloves. *Snowflakes like orange blossom of Seville in springtime. The Army of Christ takes the City of Granada.*

My father rides, clasping the same miracle-working sword that his Trastamara ancestor and his namesake, King Fernando El Santo, used when, 200 years ago, the Christians drove the Moors from the great Andalucian cities of Seville and Cordoba.

Our procession climbs up the hill and we reach the main entrance gate, the Gate of Justice, of the Alhambra Palace. We rein our horses to the side of the huge stone archway, which is five times as high as a mounted man. The two, great, bronze doors are opened. The drum roll of the marching soldiers stops.

Priests and bearers, in a cloud of incense, carry the Silver Cross through the archway first. They climb to the Torre de la Vela, the highest point on the walls and brace the cross in position for all to see.

We wait by the Gate of Justice until the Silver Cross is erected. Our soldiers cheer loudly, waving our Christian flags and banners.

Then, abruptly, complete silence.

No one knows what to do next.

Spontaneously, in unison, my father and mother dismount and sink to their knees in silent prayer. The rest of us follow them. The infantry soldiers, en masse, go down on their knees, heads bowed.

The voice of Father Cisneros fills the air, with a melodic chant in Latin, its cadences not unlike that of the *muzzein*. "Glory to God, the Father, the Son and the Holy Spirit! *Viva España!*"

We make the sign of the cross, and I see many touching the amulets or crosses they wear around their necks. I, too, touch the talisman of Merina de Cordoba tucked securely inside my bodice.

We rise, and mount our horses once again.

King Boabdil waits on the other side of the archway. He is on foot, in accordance with the protocol of surrender, with his page holding his horse just behind him. It is the same black stallion that he rode that day at the cave.

I see King Boabdil's dark eyes, accenting the paleness of his face. His face is much thinner than I remember, his cheekbones sharply edged above his beard. He wears in his turban the great ruby, holding fire in its depths. King Boabdil looks straight at me and I turn my head away, unable to meet his eyes.

Each city in Spain, whether Christian or Moorish, jealously guards the official ceremonial keys to its main gate. The City of Granada has two keys of heavy bronze, carved and ornate, each double the size of man's hand. One key represents the capital city; the other key represents the entire Moorish Kingdom of Granada. The two keys rest parallel on a turquoise brocade cushion, with tassels of gold falling from the cushion corners. The heavy weight of the keys makes the pillow sag in the middle.

King Boabdil himself takes the cushion from his captain of the guard and carefully lifts it, bearing the keys up to King Fernando, who remains on horseback. My father slides the holy sword of King Fernando El Santo back into its scabbard, takes off his glove and leans down from his saddle to touch the keys with his bare right hand. He keeps his hand on the keys, taking a deep breath, and I see his breath exhale as a cloud in the frosty air.

King Boabdil then takes the cushion to Queen Isabel and she, also on horseback, removes her glove. My mother makes the sign of the cross and caresses the keys with her fingertips.

My mother beckons to Juan to ride forward, and my brother touches the keys for the first time. Granada is now his inheritance.

I stroke Tinto's neck, keeping him quiet, as the Spanish captain of the guard removes the keys to Granada from the cushion and lashes them to his belt with a silver chain.

King Boabdil then bows formally through the archway, toward the first courtyard of the Alhambra Palace. He indicates that we – the royal family – should follow him.

I hold Tinto motionless. I am stricken with a sense of premonition. My heart beats so loud I think everyone must hear it. I am terrified to pass under the Moorish archway. *Something beyond your wildest dreams lies on the other side,* a voice whispers in my head, and I think it is the voice of Merina de Cordoba. *Through this arch lies the end of your world and your childhood. Your life will change: nothing will ever be the same again.*

My father and mother ride under the archway, then my brother, followed by Father Cisneros. Then Isabella and Catalina. Maria, smiling shyly, moves ahead. *I stop; I cannot go further.* The sun flares from behind a cloud and a sudden shaft of light strikes the wet cobblestones in front of me. The wet stones are a mirror, reflecting the sunlight directly into my eyes. I cannot see; I shake my head. *I close my eyes against the glare which shimmers like a pool of mercury.*

When I open my eyes, I see my parents and sisters and brother grouped together on the other side of the Gate of Justice, as if in an altar painting, framed by the shadowed archway. My mother frowns and makes an impatient gesture with her gloved hand for me to follow, to join them. Yet I cannot, I am anchored here. *I am the last one, the only Trastamara left beyond the arch.*

"Juana," I hear my brother's voice calling. I look across the distance that separates us, into his eyes, and the fear falls away from me. *I would follow him anywhere, through the Gate of Justice, into the Alhambra, into whatever destiny awaits us.*

✠

I maneuvre Tinto next to Juan's horse and grooms rush out to hold the horses' bridles as our family dismounts. The first courtyard is the largest, built to hold riders, but the rest of the interlacing courtyards of the Alhambra Palace we will enter on foot.

King Boabdil is our guide. He turns with a graceful bow to my parents and speaks in Castilian Spanish.

"I would ask a favour of you. My officials and I will leave the palace immediately, but, just for this one last night, could my mother and her women remain in the Alhambra's harem quarters? My mother, Princess Fatima, asks for this."

My mother hesitates, and looks to my father.

"Of course," Papa replies. He is prepared to show generosity in victory.

"Thank you, my Lord."

King Boabdil leads us into the Hall of the Ambassadors. We pause at the long, rectangular, reflecting pool, which carries the image of the building's arches in its dark water. Goldfish rise slowly and lazily to the surface. My eyes open even wider and I catch my breath, enchanted. My sisters begin whispering excitedly among themselves. Even the great halls of the Alcazar Palace in Seville, where we have lived, cannot compare with this.

King Boabdil touches his lips, as if hesitant to speak, then begins.

"There are over 300 female slaves and older concubines still living here, from my father and grandfather's reigns. In accordance with our custom, the royal wives and concubines and their women slaves, once they enter the harem of the Alhambra, are cloistered here for life. They have never left these courtyards and gardens since the day they arrived."

Mama asks him sharply, "Are they all slaves? Don't they want to be free?"

"They have known no other life than this. In the Alpujarra mountains, where I am going, I will not be able to maintain a household of this size."

"The women need not leave the Alhambra if they choose," my mother says. "If they are baptised in the Christian faith, they will be free to leave Granada to return to their families." She pauses. "However, if they wish to continue living a sheltered life here, they can become nuns. I will be endowing a Franciscan convent to be set up in the precincts of the Alhambra. Cloistered life in the convent will be much the same as they have known in the harem. Except, of course, instead of dedicating their lives to a Moorish sultan, they will be dedicating their lives to Christ."

King Boabdil nods. "Many women of my father and grandfather's time were Christian girls when they came here, captured as slaves."

"Then I pray that they can find comfort in their renewed Christian faith. In our convents the nuns live and work in a peaceful community. Some tend their herb gardens as healers. Many write illuminated manuscripts and books. Those so gifted compose and play music, and those that have the skills of the kitchen are famed for their sweet creations."

"I thank you. The harem is centered around the Courtyard of the Lions. I will send my mother the message that you have granted her request. Now, please come this way, to the treasury."

King Boabdil leads us through a maze of passages and stops before a great, bronze door. Two silent Moorish guards, armed with scimitars, stand in front of it. He commands the guards to open the door, which, because of its great weight, can only be moved inches at a time.

The large room is windowless and dark inside. King Boabdil calls for a lantern.

"My treasury. As agreed, this is now yours. You asked me to fill the room with gold and treasures to the height of a man. This I have done."

My mother bids Don Isaac Abravenel to step forward, with his assistant and his bookkeeping ledgers. "Don Isaac will accompany us," she says.

I stand at the door with my brother and sisters, peering inside the room, watching my parents and Don Isaac inch their way through a narrow passageway between the riches, which fill the room. Juan motions to me to follow him inside.

I gasp. In the flickering lantern light I see pillar after pillar, stretching the length of the room, made of stacked solid gold bars. There are dozens of large, red leather sacks overflowing with gold nuggets and hundreds of pearl-inlaid boxes opened to reveal gold bracelets, chains and earrings. I see shelves of ingots of solid silver; there is a mountain of priceless Turkish carpets and, against the wall, hundreds of bolts of the finest silk.

The room is filled with the scent of the rarest spices, worth their weight in gold: peppercorns, cinnamon and nutmegs, which spill from their finely-woven baskets. There are alabaster urns of exquisite perfumes, and Omani frankincense.

There are four huge, locked, iron chests, and King Boabdil orders the guard to open them. Inside are jewels, jewels the size of birds' eggs, and of stunning brilliance: rubies, lapis lazuli, pearls, emeralds, sapphires, diamonds. My father takes his sword and uses it as a measuring stick, levering through the jewels to reach the bottom of the chests. There are no short trays holding the jewels up. The jewels are the depth of his sword to its hilt. He nods to King Boabdil in astonishment and approval.

"All is in order."

My mother turns to her treasurer. "Don Isaac, would you please stay and begin the inventory? The king and I will see the rest of the palace."

We follow King Boabdil through the Alhambra, each hallway and courtyard garden more splendid than the one before. *Again, I wonder how he can bear to say goodbye to this place.*

Tomorrow his entourage will leave the city for the Alpujarra mountains, where a small province is granted to him by the terms of the surrender: a mountain kingdom – a vassal state to Christian Castile – between the Sierra Nevada mountains and the Malaga coast. There, he will be a regional governor, swearing allegiance to my parents, in his new capital of a rural hill village.

When we reach the palace mosque, my mother orders Father Cisneros to enter the building and bless it, turning it into our own Christian Chapel Royal. The other mosques in the city will, under the terms of the surrender, remain mosques for their Moorish communities.

Juan and I stand at the door of our newly dedicated church, and we bid King Boabdil farewell.

"Until tomorrow," he says, with the familiar graceful Arab salute I remember from our first encounter at the cave. He turns to my parents. "I will return to escort my mother and her servants and my own two wives away. They will be coming with me to the Alpujarras. I thank you for honouring my mother's request to remain for this last evening." Ex-King Boabdil and his courtiers walk through the courtyards and exit through the Gate of Justice.

Inside the mosque-church, Father Cisneros and his assistants place in the *mirab* – the Islamic niche that indicates the direction of Mecca – the statue of the Virgin Mary that graced our previous chapel in Santa Fe.

The mosque lamps remain lit, for they are treasured as the new sacristy lamps. The mosque lamps are made of beautiful coloured glass, shining in intricate geometric patterns.

I know that, in past centuries when the Moors conquered a Christian city, they would transform our churches into their mosques. The victorious Moors would take the bells from the church belltower and move them inside the building. There, they would re-hang them with chains from the ceiling, circling the bells with candle holders to make them into lamps. The bell-lamps were treasured by the Moors as the most prestigious of war trophies, and the empty belltower itself would be used as a minaret for the *muezzin*.

In our new chapel an altar is set up, covered with the cloth that my sisters Maria and Catalina had so laboriously embroidered. An ivory crucifix is set on top of the cloth.

Our family kneels down on the thick Turkish carpets that cover the floor. Father Cisneros says the first Mass here, and each of us receive Holy Communion. After Mass, my parents bid us goodnight and go alone, just the two of them, into the palace *hamman*, the Arab baths. King Fernando and Queen Isabel order that they not be disturbed for the rest of the evening, and they post sentries outside the door of the baths to insure their privacy.

During the last two years of the Granada campaign, my mother refused the luxury of using the Moorish bath houses in Seville or Cordoba. She was determined to share the hardships of her army; if her soldiers had to bathe in icy mountain streams, so would she. During the campaign, in the privacy of her tent, my mother would stand in a large, rough-cast ceramic bowl and have pitchers of cold or lukewarm water poured over her by her maids for her ablutions.

I adore going to the *hammans* in Seville and Cordoba. My nurse told me that with the Moorish conquest and re-building of the old Roman cities of Iberia, the baths became even more sensuous and elaborate. *Hammans* are beautiful buildings, with rooms of marble columns – strictly segregated into separate sections for men and for women. Scented steam drifts in clouds from pools of hot water as fountains play in each room and courtyard. There are bath attendants to massage, scrub and wash the hair of those bathing. There are relaxing rooms where the bathers lounge on couches to talk and gossip, and drink fresh fruit juices or iced sherbets.

Tonight, my mother and father will share the sensuous delights of the baths of the Alhambra.

✠

In silence, I wait while servants unroll the camp beds for me and my sisters in a sheltered alcove just off the Hall of the Ambassadors. This courtyard complex is where King Boabdil met foreign emissaries; I assume that, later, my parents will use the Hall of the Ambassadors for the same purpose. *For this first night, thank God, the foreign ambassadors are being housed in the City of Granada itself, not the Alhambra Palace. The thought of Father Adrian Boyens creeping around makes me feel ill.*

The night is cold and our sleeping alcove is heated with braziers of fragrant wood. Tomorrow, we royal sisters will move to our permanent rooms in the Courtyard of the Lions.

Juan has his quarters already assigned, and I try to slip away from my sisters to visit him.

Isabella sees me. "Juana, where do you think you are going?"

"To see Juan, I've written a poem I wanted to show him. I think he could put it to music."

"Well, don't take long, and don't go near the *hamman*. Mama and Papa have this night to themselves."

"Of course."

Isabella punches her pillow. "I'm so tired of camping out. I can hardly wait for tomorrow and my own proper bedroom at last! I'm going to choose my room first, to get just what I want."

I make a face. *Isabella can be so tiresome.*

As I walk through the Alhambra gardens, I look up at the velvet blue night sky filled with stars, where the full moon glows silver. I feel like I am floating through a dream.

In his room, Juan is seated alone and surrounded by the light of dozens of candles. He is toying with his guitar, strumming new chords. "I was trying to find the music, to evoke the beauty of the Alhambra," he says. "But what words, what music, can describe this place and what it means to me?"

He puts the guitar to one side.

I hand him the paper with my new poem. He reads it and smiles. "You've put it well. It is 'a sacred place of enchantment'."

He places my poem next to his guitar and shows me a small carved box, inlaid with intricate mother-of-pearl, Moorish, geometric patterns.

"What is it?" I ask, sitting next to him on the large floor cushions.

Juan opens the box and takes out a large ruby, holding it in front of a candle flame. In the ruby's depths are both sunrise and sunset.

"King Boabdil's jewel from his turban! His ruby!" I exclaim.

Juan hands me the jewel. "He sent it to me, secretly, by a trusted courier. He said wanted me – especially me – to have this ruby. Protocol, of course, means he should have given this personal jewel to Papa or Mama. But his message said that this is his gift to me, the heart of the Alhambra." He watches me hold the ruby in my hands, warming it, admiring the play of fire in its depths. "King Boabdil said I would treasure his jewel, his people and his Kingdom of Granada, as he tried to do."

"King Boabdil is right, you know. One day, you will be crowned King of Granada and King of all Spain. You will be the best king in the world."

He blushes as I return the ruby to him, and he puts it back in its box. Juan summons a servant and orders wine for us to drink – an exciting innovation, for we usually only drink wine at family meals. We sip our wine and listen, in companionable silence, to the tinkling music of the fountains. Somewhere in one of the distant towers, an owl hoots in the night.

"It feels strange to be the first free Christians to live here," I say.

"I feel the same." He puts down his goblet and picks up his guitar, strumming it thoughtfully. "But the Alhambra is our home now."

"Well, it's not all ours *yet*," I say, made bold by the wine.

Juan looks puzzled.

I take a long, slow sip and point my goblet in the direction of the harem quarters.

"Ah yes; King Boabdil's mother. Doña Fatima is still Queen of the Courtyard of the Lions tonight."

"Courtyard of the Lions. Good place for her. They say

she's a lioness, the most formidable woman in Andalucia."

"I thought Mama was the most formidable woman in Andalucia? Or maybe sister Isabella?" Juan laughs. "My music master Baba Hussein says that the mother is the most powerful person in a Moorish home, and a sultan's mother is the most powerful of all. He told me, 'a sultan can have wives and concubines beyond number, but only one mother'."

I pour myself another goblet of wine and recklessly drain it all in a single gulp. I toy with the stem.

"Not so fast, Juana. I will order some pomegranate juice if you are thirsty."

"No, I'm not thirsty. I've never felt better."

My brother starts to play his guitar again and I stand and dance to the music. My arms and wrists glide with the rhythm, my feet move, my body sways. I feel I could dance forever.

When Juan finishes playing, I sigh and collapse on an *almohada* floor cushion. "I'm so happy, but I can't stop thinking about Doña Fatima." I cross my hands behind my head and lie back on the cushion, looking up at the carved, painted surfaces of the ceiling above me; the intricate plasterwork glows like ivory in the candlelight. "It's going to break her heart to leave the Alhambra."

"Don Edmundo says she was the one encouraging the *jihadis* to blow up the Alhambra. Thank God it didn't happen."

I shudder. I cannot believe anyone would destroy a single stone of this exquisite place.

"Is it true that you girls will move into the harem quarters after Doña Fatima leaves?" Juan smiles. "I bet that our sister Isabella plans to be there at dawn to get the best room."

I sit upright and shake my head. "No! I will be first, for

once. I'm not going to make do with Isabella's rejects."

"How will you get there before her? Lock Isabella in the treasury?"

I stand up. I am slightly unsteady on my feet from the wine and reach out to brace myself, my palm flat against the patterned green and gold tiles on the wall. I lift my chin defiantly. "I'm going to the harem right now to find the room I want."

"Oh Juana, be serious. It's not a good idea. But if you really want to do it, I'm going with you."

"You can't come, you're a boy. Men aren't allowed into the harem. I can go there without breaking the agreement our parents made, because I'm a girl. Even if someone sees me, they'll think I'm a servant."

Juan takes a sip from his wine glass, then picks up his guitar again. "If you aren't back here by the time this sand-glass runs out, I'm coming after you, harem rules or no harem rules."

He gives me a large, brightly-burning candle, which I hold carefully in front of me as I cross the courtyard. Then I take a sharp left turn down a short corridor, cross a second courtyard and explore my way to small passage, almost hidden by jasmine vines.

At the end of the passage is a heavy, wooden door, banded with iron and blocking my way. I give it a gentle push and it opens just a fraction, enough for me to slip through.

The corridor closes around me like spilled black ink. A breeze blows out my candle. I am in complete darkness, but determined to go on. I set down the candle and feel my way along the corridor, running my hand over the textured, patterned wall tiles, my slippered feet soundless. The corridor branches to the right and I follow it, still tracing my fingertips along the wall, hoping to find another open passage. I step cautiously onto a series of floor ramps that first go up, then down. There is another long passageway, then a series of uneven steps.

I am not frightened, but feel strangely exhilarated. I see a tiny, pulsing light at the end of this corridor and approach it. When I'm closer, I see an archway framing the light and I walk through it, into a courtyard lit by the full moon overhead. I breathe in the sweet scent of winter-flowering jasmine.

The owl hooting again makes me jump. I become aware of the sound of a splashing fountain; I have reached the heart of the harem, the Courtyard of the Lions.

The moonlight paints the stones silver, and I am the only one here. *How strange,* I think. *All the women in the harem must be asleep. Their rooms are probably just off this courtyard.*

I see the circle of twelve lions of the fountain; sturdy, carved, life-sized beasts holding the granite basin on their backs, their open mouths spouting streams of water into a circular channel at their great paws. The fountain is less than twenty steps from me, but I remain in the shelter of a grove of slender, white, marble pillars; they are like the trunks of slim, graceful trees in a paradise garden. I press my cheek against the cool marble, feeling a sense of peace and tranquillity. All discontent, and the nagging challenge to push ahead of Isabella, vanish.

The circle of stone lions draw me like a magnet; in the moonlight, my shadow trails at my heels like a black silk cape. I reach the closest lion and stretch out my hand to stroke its carved granite mane; the stone feels almost alive under my fingertips. I put my hand under the crystal stream flowing from the lion's jaws, cup my palm and bend my head to drink. The water is deliciously cold, like melted snow from a mountain stream. The loud splashing of the fountain is all I can hear and I close my eyes as I continue to drink, filled with a sense of well-being, of tranquillity, of belonging.

Then my hair is grabbed and my head is slammed back sharply. *Dear God, is my neck broken?* I freeze as a woman's voice hisses, "Why are you here?"

I manage to twist slightly, and I look into an old, lined face; grey hair in a bun, the long golden tassels of her jewelled earrings quivering. I gasp, but can say nothing.

"You're one of them, aren't you?" She gives my head another shake. "Could you not allow me this last night in my own home?"

I squirm to escape, but she grips my hair even tighter. With her other hand she slaps me across the cheek, the gold bracelets on her wrists clattering. The pain brings tears to my eyes.

"Let me go," I say though clenched teeth. "Who are you?"

"Who am I? The one you and your family are going to throw out into the wilderness tomorrow."

*Doña Fatima, King Boabdil's mother.*

She weeps with rage. "Tomorrow I'm going away to some rat-infested mountain village, mud huts in the middle of nowhere." She gives my hair another tug that feels like she's pulling it from the roots. "And *you* will live in my palace, all by order of my son."

I catch Fatima's hand with both of mine and pry her bony

106

fingers loose from my hair. I pull away and step back out of her reach. "It's not my fault."

"Oh, but it is your fault. You are one of *them*, and I curse you." Fatima stands upright, facing me, and stretches out her left hand with her palm raised toward me. "I curse you!"

"No!" I make the sign of the cross against her curse, touch the gold crucifix at my neck and retreat, trying to edge around the circle of stone lions. She follows me, her eyes burning into mine.

"I wish this upon you: *may your own son one day destroy you, as my son has destroyed me.*"

"I have no son."

"Oh, but you will. One day you will." She gestures around her. "Do you find my Alhambra an earthly paradise? I did, when I was your age."

"It's beautiful," I stammer.

"But, cursed one, you will never play with your babies here in the gardens of the Alhambra. You will grow old and die, as I am condemned to die: in some poor, cold, miserable mountain village, sold out by those you trusted, betrayed by your own son."

"No!" I shout. "No! Never!" I turn and run out of the courtyard, back through the dark corridors that twist like the Minotaur's labyrinth. Doña Fatima makes no attempt to follow me. I keep running until I find my way back to Juan.

He catches me in his arms. "What happened? Are you all right?"

I choke back my sobs. I don't want to upset my brother, so I lie. "Oh Juan, I got lost in a dark corridor and a bat

107

brushed against my face, then my candle went out. So I ran back here. I never found the Courtyard of the Lions."

"Have some more wine," he says, patting my shoulder. "Pull yourself together. I'll take you back to your room. We don't want Isabella to see you upset."

We walk hand-in-hand through the courtyards. As usual, Juan charms Isabella and he kisses the sleeping faces of our two youngest sisters. I go silently to my bed.

Across the alcove, Isabella blows out her candle and the room is dark, with pale bars of moonlight filtering through the intricate wooden slats of the window.

But I can't sleep; Doña Fatima's words haunt me. *May your own son one day destroy you, as my son has destroyed me. You will never play with your babies here in the gardens of the Alhambra. You will grow old and die, as I am condemned to die, in some poor, cold, miserable mountain village, sold out by those you trusted, betrayed by your own son.*

I summon into my mind the image of Merina de Cordoba. I pray to be protected from the wrath of Doña Fatima. *My own great-grandmother, Merina de Cordoba, so beautiful, so courageous, the beloved wife and mother of Christian kings. What would she do?*

I feel a deep sense of calm settle over me. I feel inspired. *I will defy Doña Fatima's curse.* I will never have a son. I will never marry or have any children at all. I will become a nun.

✠

The next day King Boabdil comes to take his mother from the Alhambra Palace to begin their exile. His retainers wait for them, mounted, outside the Gate of Justice.

I am with my family at Mass and do not see Doña Fatima emerge from the Courtyard of the Lions, heavily veiled, walking through the gardens of the Alhambra for the last time. Outside the Gate of Justice, she and her ladies-in-waiting are helped to mount on their white riding mules, with gold-inlaid saddles and bridles.

Lord Sales is there and he tells me, later, that King Boabdil's face is wet with tears as he leaves his beloved city.

☩

King Boabdil pauses to look back at Granada one last time, and sighs. His mother, Doña Fatima, spurs her mount next to her son's, throws her veil back from hard, dry eyes and snarls at him, "Weep like a woman over what you could not defend as a man."

King Boabdil bows his head and leads what is left of his royal court to the mountains of the Alpujarras.

☩

The next day, I walk with Juan and Don Edmundo from the Alhambra Palace, up the hill to the Generalife Gardens. He tells us the story of King Boabdil's departure.

My cheeks flush crimson, but I say nothing.

My brother is angry. "How could his mother say that to him? I think King Boabdil has both courage and compassion. His first thought is for his people. His people can still live in their homes in Granada, the Moorish tradesmen continue their crafts, the scholars continue studying in their libraries, the poets can write, the musicians compose. Their mosques stay open for worship."

"True," Lord Sales says. "He did the best he could."

We sit together on a marble bench under an arbor. We are at a *mirador*, a viewing point, overlooking the city. On a frame above our heads is a tracery of bare winter vines; I can see the blue sky through the calligraphy of ink-coloured branches. In the summer, these now barren vines, carefully pruned and trained, will turn into a thick cover of emerald leaves and purple grapes – a welcome shelter from the summer sun.

A stone's throw from where we sit, I see Moorish gardeners busy trimming the tall cypress hedges.

The oldest gardener is whippet-thin, wearing a brown turban and a calf-length tunic. He whispers to one of the boys working with him; the lad stops his pruning and disappears around the corner of the high hedge. I wonder where he is going.

Lord Sales doesn't notice the gardeners, for he is staring at the view of the city below us. He continues talking to Juan. "The Moors of Granada should be grateful; they are defeated, but still have their homes. In Constantinople forty years ago, the Christian leaders refused to surrender their city to the Muslim Turks, and fought to the bitter end, street by street, house by house."

"And they lost everything," Juan says. "Constantinople is now an Islamic city." My brother respects Lord Sales as his mentor in war and in peace.

"Both Constantinople and Granada were thought invincible for centuries, but now we use new weapons – cannons and gunpowder," Lord Sales says.

Juan breaks off a stick and draws figures in the sand below our feet. "Don Edmundo, do you remember when Constantinople fell to the Turkish army?"

"I was only a little boy in England then." Lord Sales leans back and closes his eyes. "But I remember. No one alive in Christendom could ever imagine great Constantinople falling; the news hit everyone in England like the end of the world."

Juan draws a picture of a castle with his stick, then rubs it out. "Papa said in Spain they truly thought it was end of the world – just like in the Bible, in Revelations. When they heard the news of the fall of Constantinople, my grandfather said that people packed into every church in Barcelona to pray for deliverance. They believed that the victorious Turks would attack our Kingdom of Aragon next; that Turkish warships had already set sail across the Mediterranean. The Moorish Kingdom of Granada – under a different ruler – could have backed a Turkish invasion in Spain."

Lord Sales slowly opens his eyes, and looks thoughtful. "Perhaps our taking Granada means the end of the world. We Christians take Granada, just as forty years ago, the Muslims took Constantinople."

We listened intently as Lord Sales continues. "Two of the greatest cities in the world, both imperial glories, submit to the religion of their conquerors: Constantinople and Granada. It seems to me that God works like a celestial jeweller balancing his scales: so much here, so much there, and the weights continue suspended in perfect balance. The jewel of the Eastern Mediterranean – Constantinople – now Muslim, the jewel of the Western Mediterranean – Granada

– now Christian. What greater change could possibly happen next?"

Juan pauses thoughtfully, then replies. "There is the Granada Prophecy. Perhaps it will be fulfilled in our time."

Lord Sales sighs. "Spain is a land of prophecies; it's very different in England. We've never had to fight the Moors to get our country back…"

I interrupt. "And you said that in England you don't have any orange trees, or lemon trees, or sugarcane. Poor Don Edmundo, you must stay here with us." I snuggle closer to his side, as I see the gardener's boy coming from behind the hedge, approaching us.

He carries a basket covered with a white cloth. He bows before us, smiles shyly and holds out the basket.

I reach to remove the cloth, when Lord Sales shouts, "Wait!"

He uses the point of his dagger to flip the basket out of the boy's hands, sending the fruit tumbling into the dust.

The boy falls to his knees, shaking. The basket had been filled with choice, ripe pomegranates.

"It was a gift, sir," he stammers. "From Gul Baba, the head gardener."

Juan and I cry together, "Why did you do that, Don Edmundo?"

He puts his knife down beside him on the bench. "You must remember that you live among a conquered people in Granada. Trust no one; that basket might have had a poisonous snake under the cloth, or a spider with a fatal bite among the fruit. In this case, it's what it is: a gift."

Juan drops the stick he was holding and lays his hand on

the boy's shoulder. "Come, let me help you collect the fruit," he says in the Andalucian patois. The two of them gather the pomegranates and replace them in the basket, which Juan gives to me. Then my brother walks over to the group of gardeners who huddle by the hedge. I see him talking to the head gardener, and the old man kneels and kisses Juan's hands.

Juan returns to us. "I thanked Gul Baba and his gardeners for the gift and told him we will share the fruit with our sisters and parents, after we've eaten ours here at the *mirador*. I praised them for tending the gardens so beautifully, and asked them to continue their good work for me."

Don Edmundo cups a pomegranate in the palm of his hand and knifes through the tough outer skin, which is the colour of pink, speckled, amber. He hands half of it to me.

"What is your English name for this fruit?" I ask.

"Pomegranate."

"In Spanish, it's *Granada*. The symbol of this city. The best *granadas*, or pomegranates, grow here. They're delicious, aren't they?" I nibble the moist interior of the fruit, each tiny segment glistening like a miniature ruby.

Don Edmundo makes us laugh with his clumsy attempt to bite through the pomegranate's thick outer rind. He splutters, spitting out the bitter yellow pith that holds the tiny fruit segments in place. Fragments fall down the front of his doublet, leaving flecks of purple juice stains.

Juan finishes his pomegranate and tosses the rind into a patch of rough grass. He stands up. He is very still and looks around him, taking in the view of the City of Granada, the Generalife gardens and the towers of the Alhambra Palace.

"Granada is the golden treasure of Spain," he says. "I

promise both of you that as king I will safeguard the Alhambra Palace. Every monarch of Spain crowned after me will swear the same oath."

His words stun me. This is the first time I have heard my brother speak of Granada – and the Alhambra Palace – as his inheritance when he is king. I've overheard others talking about Juan's future, of course, but until today, my brother has been discreetly silent, even with me.

"Come," he says, picking up the basket of pomegranates. "Let's share the gardeners' gift with Mama and Papa."

Juan leads the way down the pathway. I brush against a tumbling great bush of rosemary, which releases its perfume into the cool breeze. *For the rest of my life, the scent of rosemary will always remind me of my brother.*

I see Gul Baba and the gardeners bow reverently to Juan as he leaves the garden.

✠

Adrian Boyens strides briskly past the guard into the courtyard where King Fernando and Queen Isabel rest. Seeing his clerical gown, the guard does not stop him.

The monarchs sit quietly side by side on silk cushions that cover a low, carved, wooden platform near the fountain. They are enjoying each other's company, listening to the music of the fountains and the birds, momentarily free of official duties.

Fernando frowns when he sees Adrian Boyens approaching. The man's eyes remind Fernando uncomfortably of a wolf tracking a wounded stag.

Father Adrian bows and addresses them in Latin, the phrases embroidered with courtier's flattery. "King Fernando, Queen Isabel, what a miracle finding you here alone! I wanted to speak to you – to thank you – and your dear chaplain Father Cisneros – for your boundless hospitality and supreme kindness to me. I find the Alhambra a Paradise on earth; I praised God when I saw your son Don Juan riding into the city, restored by God to his full health. Our prayers have been answered."

Queen Isabel crosses herself and smiles. "Our son is precious to us, and to all Spain." She gestures to Father Adrian to sit on a bench in the shade near them. He accepts with alacrity. "With your great victory over the Moors, Inquisitor Torquemada prophesies that Spain's destiny is now clear. A brilliant future lies ahead of you, and your son. Have you considered whom he will marry? He will need a steadfast and able partner to assist him with the great burdens of governing."

The king and queen glance at each other in astonishment at the Austrian ambassador's directness.

"He's still young, there will be time to find a wife." Fernando watches a quick-flying swallow dip into the fountain, still on the wing, for a drink of water.

"Of course, of course, but parents can never plan early enough for the divine gift of grandchildren. You must protect your God-given inheritance and insure the peace and security of Spain and all Christendom. How are your lovely daughters? Such paragons of charm and beauty. They will make perfect wives for fortunate bridegrooms."

Fernando raises an eyebrow.

Father Adrian takes a deep breath. "As I commended to you

at my first audience, my Austrian master, Maximilian Habsburg, has been crowned Holy Roman Emperor, the greatest title in Christendom. He has both a son and a daughter, of similar ages to your own dear children. The Duchess Margaret of Burgundy is twelve, almost thirteen. A lovely Christian girl, quite grown-up for her age; she's like a daughter to me. And, of course, the handsome young Archduke Phillipe of Burgundy."

Queen Isabel toys with her fan. "The emperor must be grateful to you for taking such good care of his children. How can he bear being separated from them? My children are always with me, wherever I go."

"You are the best of mothers, my Lady…"

Fernando sighs impatiently. "Are you going back to Austria soon?"

"I thought perhaps later this spring. First sailing to Flanders and Burgundy, then overland to Austria."

"An excellent plan," Fernando says. "Your young wards must be missing your guidance."

Isabel intercedes gently, "I have a favour to ask before you go."

"Of course, my Lady. Tell me, and I endeavor to fulfill your wishes. Anything to help." He closes his wolf-eyes in quiet satisfaction.

"Father Cisneros told me that, in Flanders, you are a friend of the great philosopher Erasmus of Rotterdam," she says.

Father Adrian blinks, startled, "Yes, my Lady." Then he lies, "Erasmus and I are the best of friends." He thinks, *Erasmus! My rival and 'bete noir'. Everyone praises his books and hail him as the genius of the New Age. What about me? Erasmus's books are printed and re-printed until the presses wear out. What sentimental tripe people want to read and believe in! I detest his milksop philosophy, about 'the goodness of princes, the power of a moral man'. Power means the strength to destroy those who oppose you. In the future, I predict that Erasmus will be forgotten dust, while the legacy of Adrian Boyens will shape the world.*

Fernando takes his wife's hand and says, "We try to get the best tutors for our son in everything – music, science, languages. Do you think Don Erasmus would come to Spain, as a philosophy tutor to Don Juan?"

"I will write him immediately," Father Adrian replies.

The queen opens her fan and studies the design on the fretwork. "I have seen these new books sent from the North; the Germans have designed an innovative machine for printing. I've read the Bible, sent by – how do you pronounce it? – Gutenberg. His new machine can create hundreds of books, on paper, quickly and cheaply. In our monastery libraries in Spain,the monks and nuns create beautiful books, but each book takes years to make: preparing the parchment, hand-lettering the manuscript, painting the coloured illustrations."

"Yes, my Lady. I think this Gutenberg machine will change everything about books. I have personally seen the new printing workshops."

"Could possibly encourage a German printer to bring his machine to Spain and begin printing books here? I want more books for my own personal collection, and I plan to establish libraries in every city in Spain."

"Of course, my Lady."

Isabel looks at her husband, smiles, and closes her fan with a quick, firm gesture, to indicate the end of the conversation with Father Adrian. "When these things are done, then we could speak again."

Father Adrian gets to his feet, unwilling to be dismissed. "Dearest, greatest sovereigns, I will write immediately to secure a printing press for you, and to contact Erasmus. " He hesitates. The mask of diplomatic politeness drops. "But, I feel compelled by God to warn you, that printed books and a Flemish philosopher cannot protect you from terrible danger."

King Fernando narrows his eyes.

Father Adrian continues. "I have spoken in Seville with the Grand Inquisitor Torquemada. He agrees with me."

Queen Isabel stares at him with a look that could turn a man into a pillar of salt. "You and Inquisitor Torquemada see danger? From what source?"

"The Jews, my Lady."

The queen makes a dismissive gesture.

"The political malignancy has spread beyond the *conversos* into the entire Jewish community. They plan to destroy Christian Spain."

Disbelief and anger surge across the king's face. Fernando squares his shoulders and steps down from the platform.

"In the Granada War, I begged Maximilian Habsburg to send us help. He did nothing when Christian Spain faced destruction from the Moors."

"With all respect my Lord, the emperor is under threat from the Turkish sultan on his own eastern border."

"So? His enemy is outside his border. We had the enemy within, the Moors ruling vast tracts of our own country. We had to bankrupt the treasuries of Castile and Aragon to free ourselves. Now, with our victory and the gold of Granada, you and Grand Inquisitor Torquemada decide we're in danger."

"My dear." The queen rises and goes to her husband's side, touching his sleeve.

He moves back from Adrian Boyens, breathing heavily.

Queen Isabel says, "Father Adrian, I think it best if you leave us now." The king and queen look at each other in silence, then watch the ambassador depart. "Let's sit down," Isabel gently urges her husband.

Fernando allows his wife to lead him back to their *almohadas*.

His anger simmers. "How dare the emperor's ambassador lecture us? Holy Roman Emperor, indeed! Maximilian Habsburg is neither Holy, nor Roman, nor an Emperor. Just a jumped-up, Austrian archduke with a rag-tag group of German dominions and some lands in Flanders and Burgundy. Maximilian *paid* the Pope for that title of Holy Roman Emperor. Instead of helping us in the Granada War, he went into debt to buy himself the imperial crown. The sooner Adrian Boyens goes back North, the better."

"Fernando, my love, we have won the Kingdom of Granda. This is ours, this is one crown the emperor will never have. We can afford to be courteous to Father Adrian." She lifts her face to her husband for a kiss. They are wrapped in a tender embrace when their son and daughter run into the courtyard, laughing, Juan carrying a basket of pomegranates.

✠

On a bright, cold day in February, I ride with my family to the Alcazaba, the Alhambra's military parade ground and barracks, for a special Mass, which will be held in the open air. Today, my brother will be crowned heir-apparent to the Kingdom of Granada; he is already heir to the Kingdoms of Castile and Aragon.

His will be crowned Prince of the Asturias. Asturias is an ancient principality, in the far north of Spain. Seven hundred years ago when the victorious Moors swept though the Iberian Peninsula, they pushed the few surviving Christians into tiny, mountainous, Asturias. The Moors did not follow, but sealed off the passes to these cold northern mountains. The Moorish generals assumed that the Christian survivors were finished as a fighting force. Asturias would be the tomb of Christian Spain.

Then came the miracle. From their mountain fastness, the dogged remnant of these Christians survived. Sustained by their faith, they began to fight back, generation after generation, town by town, city by city, century by century, until last month, when our Christian army marched into defeated Granada.

Today, Father Cisneros and a host of assisting prelates conduct the coronation. A platform is set up in front of the crowd, so all can see. At the steps leading to the platform, Juan dismounts from his horse and walks to the altar.

Standing near me and my sisters are the courtiers and the royal household, and the leading representatives of the Jewish community. There are the hereditary nobles of Leon and Castile and the elected representatives from the powerful cities of Aragon: Zaragoza and Barcelona.

I watch proudly as Juan lays his hand on the Bible and with his eyes fixed on the Silver Cross, takes his oath as Prince of the Asturias in a clear, steady voice.

He makes a solemn vow to defend Spain and the Holy Catholic Church, then he kneels to kiss the fringed edges of our parents' battle flags. He is blessed by Father Cisneros who places the princely crown of Asturias on his head. Then he rises and turns to face the crowd. He salutes the massed ranks of soldiers, walks down the steps and remounts his horse.

The shouts of acclamation are deafening.

King Fernando, Queen Isabel and Prince Juan ride past the Spanish warriors. On horseback are the knights from the Spanish orders: the Knights of Santiago, the Knights of Calatrava, the Knights of Alcantara.

There are thousands of foot soldiers, grouped in their regiments, from each part of Spain. There are the wildly-cheering men from small, rocky Asturias itself; seafaring men from Galicia, sun-burned frontiersmen from the dry mesas of Extremadura, men from the rich orchards of Valencia, men from the Andalucian cities of Seville, Cordoba and Huelva; men from Castilian cities of Toledo and Burgos. Many of their families are here, too. The soldiers will get land grants and settle on conquered Moorish lands.

The sun shines on the face of our strong, handsome, young prince. The light reflects off the gold circlet of his simple crown, like a halo against his dark hair. *"Viva!"* The shout rises. *"Viva Don Juan! Viva El Principe!"*

My eyes fill with tears of joy. I look up to the tops of the walls surrounding the Alcazaba. I blink away my tears and see men standing on the ramparts of the fortress, outlined against the sky. It is Lord Sales and his English archers, cheering as they wave their longbows. It is their triumph, too.

✠

I follow my mother as she strides through the Courtyard of the Myrtles; I have to skip every few steps to keep up with her. She turns abruptly down a corridor and I nearly trip over her heels. She is preoccupied, for she has an appointment with Don Isaac Abravanel, the royal treasurer, to go over the accounts. I hope to intercept her first, with a private moment to tell her about my new vocation to become a nun.

*Alas, I see there will not be time.* Ahead of us, Don Isaac waits by the doors of the treasury. He bows formally, wishing my mother good day and greeting me with cheerful affection.

"What are you studying today, Lady Juana?"

"Poetry. With my brother."

"Just a moment. I have something for you." Don Isaac searches in the large leather satchel he is carrying and draws out a book. I see it is an old book, with a worn embossed green leather cover and pages of parchment. The new books made by printing presses have pages of paper.

He shows it first to my mother for her approval, then turns to me. "This is written by the Sufi poet Ibn Zamrak, praising the beauties of Granada, and the calligraphy is by Abu Malik. I purchased it from a Moorish noble who sold his library before leaving."

I eagerly take the volume. The poems are simple couplets, easy enough for me to read in hispano-Arabic. I thank Don

Isaac, sit down on a nearby wooden bench and open the pages immediately. The poems are enchanting.

I hear Don Isaac say to my mother, "God gives us the blessing of children, but only God knows what direction life will take them."

"Especially a girl like my Juana, determined only to follow her heart. She is the best scholar of all my daughters, but can be wild and stubborn sometimes."

I hear my mother's remark, but refuse to look up from my reading.

Don Isaac continues, "Children can cause their mothers many sleepless nights." He hesitates. "My wife's sister has such a child… well, no longer a child, but a young man. A mother's concern is ageless."

"What troubles her?"

"Her son has disappeared. He was taken by the Inquisition in Seville, for questioning."

I look up in alarm. My mother lays a comforting hand on Don Isaac's sleeve and they walk away from me.

"Perhaps, if inquiries could be made…"

The guards at the treasury doors stand aside to let them pass, their armor clattering and pikes hammering on the stone floor.

"I understand a mother's love for her son. I think perhaps Inquisitor Torquemada grows too powerful in Seville, he has been left on his own too long during the war. I will do what I can to help," my mother says. "Tell me, Don Isaac, is your nephew a Jew, or a *converso*?"

"A *converso*, my Lady."

✠

The weather continues cold and I drape a warm, woolen shawl over my shoulders. Today an icy rain pours down on the Alhambra Palace, leaving a glaze of water over the marble courtyards that are open to the sky.

In his study, Juan stands next to a table, his hands holding down a large map that nearly covers the table's surface. By his side is a youth, slightly younger than Juan, dressed in a royal page's uniform.

"Juana, come and look at this." My brother's eyes shine.

The page blushes crimson as he makes an awkward, formal bow. He is thin, and gangly in his formal clothes. His face is pock-marked; he must have been badly scarred by the smallpox when he was younger.

"This is Diego Columbus," Juan says. "His father is the one we nicknamed 'the Map Man', you remember him?"

I nod politely to Diego and kiss my brother on both cheeks in greeting. *So, Diego is the son of the Genoese mariner.*

I remember, last year, Lord Sales pointing the master mariner out to me at Santa Fe. He was a tall man, tense with waiting day after day in my parents' crowded audience hall, his rolls of maps and charts clutched to his chest, jostling with the other petitioners for a chance to catch the royal eyes. Petitioners swarmed to court like wasps to an overripe pear.

Lord Sales had told me, "Christopher Columbus, that's what he calls himself. He came to England to try to talk King Henry Tudor into financing his voyage. He had a plan to sail west to India, across Atlantic Ocean." He shrugged. "Nobody's ever done *that* before, and returned to tell the tale. King Henry turned him down. So Columbus went back to Spain from England, empty-handed, working his way home as navigator on the ship that brought me and my archers here. Sad, really. I think Columbus tried to sell his idea to every King in Christendom, and no takers."

My attention comes back to the present when Juan taps an index finger on the map. "Papa turned Columbus down. Mama told him that she might consider his idea. But only after taking Granada."

"Rejection broke my father's heart. He gave up and started walking back to La Rabida – that's the monastery where the Franciscan monks give us refuge."

"But why are you still in Granada?" I ask.

"Your mother said I could be one of her pages. I can write, and run errands. It is a relief for my father, because I get food and a roof over my head for the winter and a small allowance. It is one less worry for him."

"And he left you one of his maps?

"This is a copy I made of one."

Diego's hand of penmanship is very good. In the margins, the map is embellished with drawings of fire-breathing dragons and scaly sea monsters. He puts his index finger on a sketch of a Moorish castle in the top right hand corner.

"See, here is Granada, and if you follow the Guadalquiver river from the mountains to the sea, it goes through Cordoba, then Seville and then out to the sea at Cadiz."

I look at the map with renewed interest.

"And here, far to the west of Cadiz, on the Atlantic coast, is La Rabida, the Franciscan monastery where the monks have been so kind to us."

"And what's this?" I point to a squiggly line of dark blue by the monastery.

"That's the Rio Tinto river, with its port towns of Palos and Moguer; the ships sail from there out into the Atlantic Ocean."

I lean back from the table. "Is that where the sun sets into the sea? I've heard that it's the end of the world."

Juan thoughtfully brushes his fingertips across the empty spaces of the map beyond Palos and Moguer. "Diego says there is everything beyond that. I believe so, too."

"I know my father is right," Diego says. "The queen said she would consider his project again, after the Granada War was over. But perhaps she has forgotten us."

"Don't lose heart, Diego." Juan says. "I will talk with my mother."

✠

"Enough of this fiesta," Queen Isabel says, laughing and clapping her hands. She hurries everyone out of her private study: ladies-in-waiting, Father Cisneros, my brother and sisters. We are still singing and joking, enjoying the mood of the morning's light-hearted gathering, but now my mother needs to work. For this she wants to be alone.

She calls for the ledger of her accounts and the box of official documents waiting for her approval. She settles into her favourite worn camp chair, with a cushion supporting her back and the *brazero* underneath providing warmth for her feet. On the top of the massive oak table her writing quills are cut and laid in order, like a battalion of soldiers. She lifts the top off the heavy, gold inkwell.

Juan and I linger, the last ones out the door. "Mama, I have composed some new music," he says. "Would you like me to play the guitar for you while you work?"

"That would be wonderful, my angel." She never looks up or breaks her concentration, studying the first page of the stack of documents in front of her.

"May I stay and finish my embroidery?" I say.

At this, Mama raises one eyebrow in astonishment and pauses. *Juana, doing her needlework without having to be nagged?*

"The light is so good by the window," I say defensively as I plump up the cushion to sit near the window. I make a great flourish of threading the needle; when Mama's concentration returns to her papers, Juan catches my eye and winks.

For the next hour, as the sand-glass on her desk drains from one globe into its twin, Juan plays his guitar, caressing the strings. I find myself lost in the music and my embroidery threads flow easily into their proper patterns, unlike the times past when I fight them into knots.

Mama puts down her quill and raises her hands above her head, stretching the cramped muscles of her back and shoulders. She smiles and taps her foot to the tune of Juan's song.

Juan, still strumming chords of the music, speaks gently. "Mama, do you remember the Genoese mariner, called Christopher Columbus?"

"Mmmm... yes, I think so. Was he one of the petitioners at Santa Fe? So many people want things from me."

"You appointed his son one of your pages. His name is Diego and I've been talking to him, Mama."

"Whatever about?"

127

Juan makes a flourish of strings, his fingertips pressing the guitar's fretwork. "It's about his father's plan to sail to India across the Atlantic Ocean; a new way to the treasures of the East. Bolts of silk and shiploads of spices for you, Mama."

Our mother shifts the paper in front of her. "You know we have silk merchants right here in Granada. But the spices are a problem – so expensive! And the Venetian spice traders warn me that they plan to double their prices this summer. I might talk to Diego about this later, but I'm too busy now, my angel."

"Just five minutes, Mama."

She sighs. "Where is this friend of yours?"

Juan puts down his guitar and goes to the door of the study. I pretend to keep busy with my needlework, but I know Juan and Diego's plan.

Juan opens the door and Diego – who was waiting just outside – enters. He makes a formal bow to our mother. "My Lady."

Mama holds her hand out for him to kiss and says gently, "Ah yes, the master mariner's son."

Diego swallows and stares up into the *media-naranja* ceiling, as if he is memorising the patterns of the Moorish carved plasterwork. The fountain tinkles in the garden courtyard and a songbird begins to trill.

His voice trembles when he gets the courage to speak. "My Lady, may I be so bold as to remember my father to you? You are his last hope, the only one who can help him."

Juan leans over the back of Mama's chair, draping his arms affectionately around her neck and pressing his cheek to hers. "Mama, poor Master Mariner Columbus has no money left.

He even had to sell his horse. He is walking all the way back to Palos in despair. He thinks you've forgotten him."

Diego kneels in front of the queen and presses his open hand over his heart. "My Lady, I believe in my father, and his dream of sailing West to India. There are *marineros* in the ports of Palos and Moguer who are ready to go with him, but he can't pay them. There is no money to charter ships for his voyage."

Mama studies the boy kneeling before her. Juan continues to lean over her shoulder, his arms circling her neck, and she clasps his hands in her own.

"Juan, my angel, what do you think?"

"I've studied the maps. I'm sure it will work."

"Then summon Don Enrique de Leon for me."

"I'll do it, Mama," I say. I know Don Enrique, he is the captain of the royal couriers. I jump up, and my embroidery tumbles into a heap on the floor. I run out of the door, skirts flying.

When I return with the captain, Juan is standing next to Diego, in front of my mother.

"Juana, please come here," she summons me. She touches her necklace, its clasp at the back of her neck. "Could you unfasten this for me?"

I release the intricate latch. It is a lovely necklace, my mother's favourite, which she calls her 'Necklace of the Twelve Cameos'. Its thick golden chain links the lapis lazuli cameos of twelve Roman emperors, each individually framed in gold and circled with pearls.

Mama holds the necklace in her hands, running her fingers over the jewels.

"Don Enrique. You will take this necklace as surety to Don Abraham Seneor, my banker in Seville. He holds other jewels of mine, which he is to use to raise the money needed."

At her desk, she reaches for a freshly-sharpened quill and writes on a stiff sheet of official parchment.

To the citizens of the illustrious towns of Palos de la Frontera, and Moguer, in the province of Huelva. The town councils are hereby commanded to prepare two sailing caravels, and crews, for the quest of the Atlantic. I guarantee payment. God be with you.
Yo La Reina

She signs the document, *Yo La Reina* – I the Queen – and presses her seal into the red wax.

She looks at us. "Don't mention this to your father. He was firm about turning Columbus down. He said he wouldn't invest a single *maraveda* in this plan." Mama raises her chin defiantly. "So Master Mariner Columbus sails under the flag of my own Kingdom of Castile." She puts her arm around my brother. "Remember that it will be *your* Kingdom of Castile one day, Juan, my angel. This voyage is your inheritance."

She looks kindly at Diego. He seems stunned, unable to speak.

"Diego, you will leave Granada and find your father on his road to Palos. Tell him to prepare to sail. Don Enrique will accompany you."

Tears well up in Diego's eyes. "I will ride at once. Thank you, my Lady, thank you."

"After your father sails, you must come back to Granada. Together we will wait for him."

Diego and Don Enrique bow their way out the door. Mama fingers the unadorned collar of her gown, where her 'Necklace of the Twelve Cameos' once rested.

"No one has sailed beyond the Azores and survived," she says almost to herself. "But God can work miracles."

She reaches out and caresses Juan's face. "I can risk my jewels, if the *marineros* of Palos and Moguer are willing to risk their lives. The only thing I cannot risk is you, my son. You are all the world to me."

I hug closer to Juan's side. *He is all my world, too.*

✠

My sister Maria and I sit on cushions near the arched window, in our shared room called 'the Courtyard of the Two Sisters'. When I look out the window, I see a sharp drop down the Alhambra hill to the Rio Darro. Opposite, our view is of the steep hill of the Albaicin quarter, and the almond trees among the buildings have burst into the white blossom of February.

The flowering trees remind me of the tale of the Moorish prince and his Christian bride; the story I shared with King Boabdil. I wonder if he stood at this very window as a boy, and my heart aches at the thought of him. *Do the almond trees bloom at this time of year in the stark mountains of the Alpujarras?*

Maria plays with three white kittens, tumbling about in their basket; she adopted them when the women of the harem left them behind. Her little dog is growling jealously nearby, and Maria is trying to gently encourage Chica to make friends with the kittens.

*Amazing! Maria is having success in the endeavor.* Maria adores her pets, and she loves babies. Whenever any of the maidservants has a new baby to nurse, Maria is always there, begging to be allowed to hold and cuddle and play with the infant. She hates going on family hunting trips, and I know she secretly feeds her hunting falcon so many tidbits that the bird – overweight and content – never even leaves her glove to fly after game.

We watch the newly-arrived swallows darting around, coming right though the window, seeking places to build their little mud nests up in the carved eaves of the ceiling. The Moorish maids tut-tut and try to discourage the birds from nesting by prodding them with twigs tied to long poles.

"Leave the swallows, please," Maria says. "It's good luck to have swallows nesting in a house." The Moorish maids roll their eyes and leave us, grumbling. The nesting birds and their fledglings will make a mess of droppings over the floor, which the maids will have to mop up all summer.

Maria and I share this room. Isabella has indeed claimed the biggest and best room, just off the Courtyard of the Lions, but I don't care. I prefer this room, which has the most beautiful view across the narrow valley. Isabella's quarters suit her as a future Queen of Portugal, and the next biggest suite of rooms is taken by little Catalina, the Princess of Wales.

My parents have the grandest apartment in an adjacent courtyard of the palace. They are holding endless conferences with their advisors. Many of the officers and knights of the

Christian army will return to their estates in Aragon and Castile, while others are taking huge new estates in the Granada countryside.

Lord Edmund Sales is awarded a big property near Marbella, called *Torremolinos*, as a reward for his military service, along with a small fortune in gold. After four years of service in Spain, the company of English archers is disbanded and the men are richly paid off. Some of the English archers say they will stay in Spain, but most sail back to England. Don Edmundo insists that Spain is his home now.

The Condesa de Moya, Doña Beatriz, recovers slowly from her wounds. She has her own secluded quarters in the Alhambra Palace. Lord Sales is more attentive to Doña Beatriz than ever, always bringing her maid small gifts to give to her. She firmly refuses to see him, or to allow anyone but her women friends into her rooms.

✠

The ladies of the Moorish harem who chose to stay and are baptised, re-affirm their faith as Christians. With my mother and sisters, I stand as godmother at the ceremony. Many younger girls have chosen to become novices in the Franciscan order of nuns; my mother has endowed a convent in the Alhambra Palace complex.

"Mama," I say as I watched the Franciscan sisters depart the chapel. "I think I would like to become a nun."

"You, Juana?" My mother looks at me, surprised. "This is news to me. Why do you want to become a nun?"

"I love reading, I write poetry and I love music. If I am a

nun, this is what I will spend my life doing. To the greater glory of God, of course. I can live here in the Alhambra."

"We will see, you are young yet. Pray for guidance."

✠

In March, we commemorate Semana Santa, Holy Week. From Palm Sunday to Easter, Christian processions file through the streets. This is first time since, centuries ago, the first Christian inhabitants carried statues of the Virgin and the crucified Christ openly through the city. It was forbidden when Granada was under Muslim rule.

At the same time as Easter, Sephardic Jewish families celebrate Passover in Granada. Moises Sanchez shares the Passover feast with his family; he has been promoted to royal falconer, and will soon marry a Jewish girl from Seville. The family of Doctor Lorenzo Badoc, our royal physician, and the family of Don Isaac Abravanel, royal treasurer, attend the new synagog in Granada. Don Isaac and his wife Sara gratefully receive the news that their *converso* nephew, Gregorio, has been released from his detention by the Inquisition in Seville. The queen's intervention is successful.

The Jewish community cherishes Granada as their triumph; it was their acumen as financiers which kept the Christian army going forward to victory. Aristocratic Sephardic families claim direct descent from the biblical King David and their special ties with the Spanish Christian royal court give them both protection and prestige.

They see the shadow of the Inquisition over the *conversos*, but their leaders assure them that the observant Jewish community remains safe under King Fernando and Queen Isabel.

It is the calm before the storm.

✠

From the Alhambra, Adrian Boyens writes to Maximilian Habsburg, lauding his accomplishments. He signs a contract with a German printer to bring his printing press to Spain and begin work. With less enthusiasm, Adrian Boyens asks one of his staff in Flanders to contact Erasmus; he thinks: *hopefully, he'll have already taken a position somewhere else in Europe.*

Father Adrian avoids the king, but attaches himself to the queen and Prince Juan with the tenacity of a *percebe* limpet on a wave-lashed rock.

I am alone with Juan when my brother asks me, "Why do you dislike Father Adrian so much? Whenever he comes into a room, you walk out. You never speak to him."

I shrug. "I don't like the way he looks at me. He only pretends to be friendly. I think he's up to something."

"Oh Juana, that's not true. Father Adrian is kind, really, once you get to know him. I think that he's a very humble man, and he's so grateful for everything we've done for him. We've been playing chess; he's very good, and I'm learning a lot about strategy." A faint blush darkens his cheekbones. "He's been telling me about the emperor's daughter Margaret. He says she's very pretty and agreeable, and not yet promised in marriage."

"What?" I narrow my eyes and hiss, "Don't tell me you've

fallen for Margaret?" I say her name with an exaggerated English pronunciation.

"Poor Margaret Habsburg is an orphan, just like her brother Philippe."

"Only half-orphans. Their father is still alive, even if he lives in a different country. And their dead mother, the Duchess of Burgundy: didn't you hear? She was killed in an accident, a hunting accident, when they were small. It happened when she was out with her husband and her advisor, Father Adrian. Some people said it wasn't an accident at all."

"Now that is just evil gossip."

"And have you heard the other gossip? That Father Adrian is scheming his way into our confidence, to get you to marry Margaret and Maria to marry Phillipe."

"It's all talk. Mama and Papa will do what is best for us."

"Mama and Papa married for love."

"They'll never force any of us to marry against our wishes," my brother says. "I don't see any harm in Father Adrian. He keeps trying to make friends."

"You see good in everyone, but I don't trust him. Don Edmundo doesn't trust him, either. I wish Don Edmundo was here."

"I miss him, too. But he vowed to go to the north of Spain, to walk the Camino de Santiago and make the pilgrimage to Compostela, after Granada was won. He'll be back in a month or two." My brother sees how upset I am, and tries another tack.

"Look, when I was playing chess Father Adrian brought these sweets, made to a recipe of his own country. Would you like one?"

I turn up my nose. "I'd sooner eat pig swill. You didn't touch any of those things, did you?"

He shrugs. "Father Adrian ate from the box first."

I grab the box of sweets from him and flounce angrily out of his room. "I'm going to throw this away."

Juan sighs and calls after me, "You'll become a wonderful nun, Sister Juana, if you keep acting like this." I did not see it, but he has one of the sweets in his hand. After I leave, he examines it carefully, then pops it into his mouth and returns to reading his book.

When I return to my own room, I lean far out of my window and shake the sweets from their box, watching them bounce down the hill into the rocks and shrubs far below. I see a scavenging trio of dogs meandering past. The dogs eat the scattered sweets and I watch them carefully, to see if if they drop down with fits. Nothing. I hurl the box out of the window.

Everything returns to normal.

✠

Two nights later, Juan comes down with a high fever. Doctor Badoc is summoned, our parents hovering anxiously in attendance. This setback comes frighteningly close to Juan's illness of four months ago. It causes great alarm, for until now my brother has always been blessed with good robust health.

We Trastamaras are a sturdy family. My father has suffered serious wounds in battle, but recovered. My mother gave birth to her children in different cities across Spain and was up and about within days, back to her work. Sister Isabella is too thin, but that is because she never likes to eat.

Our family physician since the year before Juan's birth, Doctor Badoc has successfully tended us through our childhood ailments of measles and mumps. His insistence on pure drinking water means we are untouched by typhoid or dysentery. We all contracted the mild cowpox, rather than the terrible scarring smallpox. Doctor Badoc says this was because of our close contact with the herds of cattle that are driven from camp to camp. Under Doctor Badoc's care, our active childhood mishaps of falls from horses, minor bruises and burns, sprains and cuts are healed and we young Trastamaras have clear complexions and straight, strong limbs.

*I feel uneasy. My great fear is that my brother's health is weakened by his earlier illness, when he was caught in the storm searching for me.* I hover guiltily around his sickroom.

One of the English archers described the English sweating sickness to the doctor, and I wonder if Juan has somehow caught this. But Doctor Badoc says no, it is not the English sweating sickness, it is something he has never seen before.

Juan is dry and pale, and does not seem to know where he is.

His eyes suddenly open wide, unseeing, and his body contorts to the point when it seems his backbone will break. Then he lapses into unconsciousness.

*This cannot be happening. The vivid nightmare engulfs me, dark and powerful, the battle on the ship in the ocean storm, and my brother clinging to life.* My mother orders that the miracle-working relic of San Pancracio is brought to place on his chest, but nothing changes. Our chaplain, Father Cisneros, gently advises my parents that the last rites should be administered. He takes the holy oil and begins the Sacrament of Extreme Unction.

I see a page enter the room and press a note into my mother's hand. She unfolds the paper, and her eyes widen as she reads it. Without a word, she runs from the room.

✠

The note is from Adrian Boyens. He stands in the shadows near the altar of the chapel, lit only by the sacristy lamp. "My Lady, you have not allowed me to be at Prince Juan's bedside."

"My husband said…"

He silences her with a raised hand. "You have Jewish doctors tending Prince Juan; they cannot restore his health. I can."

She clasps her hands together, so tightly that her knuckles turn white. "If my son dies, chaos follows for Spain and for the world. It has been foretold. It is the prophecy. Ask me anything, and I will do it."

"Listen to me. I have told you before that Spain is the last country in Christendom still harbouring Jews. *If you banish them, your son will be saved.* Will you let me tend him?"

The queen bites her lip and nods.

A breathless page appears, "My Lady, the king says to return to the prince's room at once."

The queen flees from the chapel, running down the corridors of the Alhambra to her son's side. Father Adrian shadows her.

✠

My father is astonished to see Father Adrian enter the room. I see him as a terrifying apparition. *The nightmare: a priest rushes across a ship's deck, I think he is going to save my brother...*

My mother falls to her knees at Juan's bedside and throws her arms over the coverlet. Juan's body is motionless beneath the red silk bed covering, his face pale as the white linen pillow. The coverlet is embroidered in gold thread with the symbols of the Kingdoms of Castile and Aragon and Granada. My mother's hands tear at them, cutting her fingers on their spiky sharpness and ripping the gold threads to pieces.

Father Cisneros says softly, "Prince Juan is at peace with God. Let his sisters kiss him goodbye."

"No!" my mother screams.

She rises and grabs Father Adrian's sleeve. "Save my son, I beg you. I will do what you ask."

Father Adrian pushes Father Cisneros out of the way and takes his place at Juan's bedside. He glares at Doctor Badoc and orders him out of the room.

Father Adrian turns to us. "Leave me alone with Prince Juan. You must trust me, if you wish him to live."

Reluctantly, we file out of the door and Father Adrian shuts it behind us. We gather in a semi-circle outside on our knees, praying, for what seems like an eternity.

Father Adrian opens the door. "Come. All will be well."

My parents rush back into the room. My sisters and I tiptoe in behind them. Juan's face is normal, his chest rises and falls with easily-drawn breaths. I kiss his forehead; his skin is soft and fragrant.

I watch my mother again kneel by Juan's bedside, and my father kneels next to her.

I look back to the doorway. Father Adrian Boyens stands silhouetted against the light, his wolf-eyes glowing with triumph. The Jews of Spain will pay for my brother's deliverance.

✠

On the last day of March, the Edict of Expulsion hits the Spanish Jewish community like an earthquake. The edict demands that the Jews be baptised as Christians, or else leave Spain by the 31st of July, 1492.

Jew, Christian and Moor alike are stunned by the news. There has been no whispered gossip beforehand, no confrontation, no ominous weeks of rising tensions with the Spanish Christians. One day, *conviviencia*; the next, the day of doom. The document of the Edict of Expulsion is drawn up; it needs only the signatures of the king and queen. *For the Jews, four months to decide your future: become a converso or go into exile.*

The edict does not affect the Moors of Granada, as they have been granted safety by the terms of King Boabdil's surrender.

Doña Sara Abravanel runs from their Alhambra apartment through the courtyard to her husband's treasury office. "Surely this cannot be true?" she weeps. "Perhaps they want us to pay higher taxes? Spain has been our home, our own promised land of Sephard, for 1000 years."

Don Isaac tries to comfort her. *Sara and I are too old to move,* he thinks, *and too old to change. Perhaps something can yet be done, if I talk with the king and queen.*

✠

I stand silently alongside my brother and sisters, next to our parents' thrones in the Hall of the Ambassadors. I see Father Adrian Boyens, standing next to Inquisitor Torquemada, among the crowd of courtiers and priests gathered to witness the signing of edict by the sovereigns. The Grand Inquisitor has journeyed from Seville to Granada to be here.

Father Adrian and Inquisitor Torquemada exchange frowns when Don Isaac Abravanel is granted permission to formally address the court.

I stare at the Turkish carpet beneath my feet. *If I concentrate on the flowers,* I think, *the lovely pattern of flowers woven into the carpet, Mama and Papa will listen to Don Isaac. They will not sign the edict and force the Jews to make the terrible choice between conversion or exile.*

As the leader of the Jewish community, Don Isaac speaks powerfully, touching our hearts, urging a postponement of the edict. Most of the Christian courtiers nod in agreement with his reasoning. There should be more time for discussion, before ripping apart the centuries-old fabric of Spain's *conviviencia*, 'the living together'.

Don Isaac concludes his plea. "Queen Isabel, King Fernando, please allow us more time to consider the edict."

On behalf of the Jewish community, Don Isaac offers the Christian monarchs 30,000 *maravedis* of gold for a judicial reprieve.

I raise my head to watch my father. The king stirs uneasily on his throne and seems about to agree. Then my mother looks at him. He coughs, and remains silent.

Into the ominous quiet, Inquisitor Torquemada rushes

forward to the table where document of the Edict of Expulsion rests. The edict is weighted with official seals, waiting for the royal signatures. The Grand Inquisitor tears the crucifix from the gold chain around his neck and hurls it on top of the document. He glares at King Fernando.

"So, you hesitate. Why? Is it the money they offer you? Judas Iscariot sold out Jesus Christ for thirty pieces of silver. Now the King and Queen of Spain will sell out Our Lord for 30,000 *maravidis*."

My mother, pale as parchment, rises from her throne. She walks to the table and signs the document, for her Kingdom of Castile. She returns to her throne. After several long uneasy minutes, my father rises and signs for his Kingdom of Aragon. He throws the quill to the floor and strides from the hall, grim-faced, looking neither right nor left. Queen Isabel remains, alone, seated next to her husband's empty throne. The Order of Expulsion becomes the law of Spain.

✠

I stumble, blinded by tears, back to my room. Everything looks the same, yet nothing will ever be the same again. I go to the niche near my bed, where I keep the jewelled portrait of Merina de Cordoba. I long to hold her portrait in my hands, to feel again the comfort and spiritual protection of my great-grandmother.

I stare at the empty niche in horror. The jewel is gone. *What happened? Where is it?* I check through my bedding, and the chest where my clothes are stored. I call the maids: no one has seen it. *But someone must have taken it!* I call for the guards, I frantically ask my sisters: what has happened to the portrait? *Has a thief stolen it? Are they, even now, breaking up the jewel, smashing the cameo to retrieve the rubies that line the edge? Or has someone else taken it, knowing its provenance and meaning?*

The questions will haunt me the rest of my life.

It is the most precious gift my father has ever given me. He entrusted me with his talisman, to keep it safe. Now it has disappeared. I am sobbing when I tell Papa of my loss. He seems resigned. "It's gone, *querida*," he says, hugging me. My father never again speaks of his *converso* grandmother, Maria de Cordoba. Never again will I hear him praise my resemblance to the one he called the most beautiful woman in the world.

When Juan attempts to talk to our mother about the edict, urging her to reconsider, Mama is deaf to his pleas. "It had to be done," she tells him coldly. "I have my reasons. Don't ask me about it, ever again."

Later, I creep to Juan's room to discuss the edict with him. Behind the closed doors that I pass on the way, I hear weeping.

"What will become of our friend Moises?" I ask. "And Doctor Badoc and his family?" Juan sits with his head in his hands, unable to look at me. As much as I long to comfort him, my anger drives my words. "What will Don Isaac and Doña Sara Abravanel do? And Don Abraham Seneor?"

"Quiet, Juana, stop shouting."

"I'm sorry, but I can't bear it. How can Mama and Papa be so cruel?"

"I don't think they see it as being cruel. They don't want Don Isaac and Moises and Doctor Badoc to leave Spain, they just want them to be baptised and stay with us. Life will continue as it always has."

"So you think they will become *conversos*?"

"I spoke to Rabbi Jacob Santangel, Moises' uncle. He's telling people to get baptised so they can stay in Spain. He says that a forced baptism is not legally valid. Other rabbis are telling them to pack their bags and let the Kingdoms of Spain fall to pieces without them."

✠

Shortly after the Edict of Expulsion is signed, Father Adrian Boyens returns to the North. He decides not to sail but to take the longer overland route, traveling by mule train, with an armed entourage and the blessing of the Inquisition, across Castile. He takes the pass through the Pyrenees mountains and across the border into France.

In Burgundy, he inspects his ward Archduke Phillipe's inheritance, then continues further north to Phillipe's dominion of Flanders. He is re-united with both Phillipe and Margaret in the city of Lille. Assured that all is well with his charges, he goes to Austria to report to their father, Maximilian Habsburg. In his documents case, Adrian Boyens carries a secret agreement from the Spanish monarchs to begin preliminary negotiations for two betrothals.

✠

In late spring, in May, I drift listlessly through the courtyards of the Alhambra. The palace is strangely silent, haunted by the empty places of our absent Jewish friends and retainers. *My only consolation is that Father Adrian has left Spain and returned to the North, his terrible objective achieved. I hope he stays there forever.*

Don Isaac Abravanel and many senior Jewish courtiers leave Granada and return to their home cities to consider the edict: *to be baptised, or not? To leave their Spanish life for an unknown exile?*

Don Isaac and Doña Sara return to Seville, to their family home and the home of their grown children and many grandchildren. There they will decide.

✠

For the first time ever, Juan rebels against our mother's wishes. Papa wants my brother, as Prince of the Asturias, to go on his first independent royal progress this summer.

"As prince, he needs to get to know the powerful families of Andalucia. He will need their support to rule Spain when he is king," Fernando says.

Isabel frowns and refuses. She wants to keep Juan by her side.

"Our son worries too much about the edict," Fernando argues. "Traveling will distract him. Let him go to Seville to celebrate his saint's day. The Duke of Medina Sidonia has invited him on a hunting trip to the Coto Doñana. It will be better for Juan to be out in the countryside."

Mama stubbornly says no, but my brother sides with Papa. *Time to cut the apron strings.*

I beg to go with Juan, and my father agrees. "Perhaps a

change of scene will make you forget becoming a nun," he says.

Juan's spirits lift as we prepare to go to Seville, the city of his birth and baptism. I have fallen in love with Granada, but he remains faithful to Seville.

On the road, we encounter Jewish refugees, their city clothes travel-stained and their feet blistered in their once-elegant shoes. They trudge the dusty country roads to the coast, to the ships which will take them into exile. Juan reins in his horse and orders our entourage pull over to the side of the road to allow a Jewish family to pass. I see my brother's face darken in sorrow and shame as he watches them.

In spite of the edict, we ride across an Andalucian countryside that continues in its timeless rhythm. Flocks of sheep and goats, tended by solitary shepherds and their dogs, graze in the *dehesa*. Oxen are yoked to the water wheels, the water splashing, bucket after bucket, to fill the irrigation channels.

On the road, mule trains transport bales of goods, and donkeys carry nets of hay so large that the only thing to be seen are the animals' legs beneath the load.

Farm workers harvest the rich wheatfields of the Guadalquivir river valley. Red poppies and blue rosemary ruffle in the breeze under the gnarled olive trees. The heat of the sun brings out the tangy scent of white cistus blossoms.

Nearing the main gate of Seville's city walls, a huge festive crowd comes out to welcome us, with music and singing, drinking and dancing. Juan is adored by the *Sevillanos*, for he is their native-born son, their special prince. "When he is king," they say proudly, "Seville will be his home, the capital city. One of our own, a *Sevillano*, will rule all of Spain."

In Seville, we move into the Alcazar palace adjacent to the cathedral. Entering the inner courtyard, I kick off my boots and wade barefoot into the coolness of the tiled fountain pool. This palace was our military headquarters during the Granada War, the home of our ancestors for 200 years, ever since King Fernando El Santo conquered this city from the Moors.

"Which of our ancestors do you prefer," I ask my brother as I splash in the water. "King Pedro the Just, King Fernando the Wise, or King Fernando the Saint?"

The question makes my brother laugh. "Does a king have to have a nickname?" he asks, then grows serious. "What do you think they will call me?"

"King Juan the Beloved," I reply without hesitating. "I think that's better than being just, or wise, or even a saint."

"I want to be a good king, Juana. I want the Kingdoms of Spain to be united, to be one great nation. I care about all our people. I would never have expelled the Jews."

I stop splashing in the fountain and stare at him. "Do you think Mama and Papa are wrong about the edict?"

He nods: *yes*. I am shocked. I have always thought of our parents as invincible and all-knowing. To cover my confusion, I change the subject. "What do you think they will call me, as the king's twin sister?"

"Juana la Belleza," he says smiling. "Juana the Beautiful."

*My dearest brother, how I longed for that wish of yours to become true. A beauty, yes, I would become a beautiful woman: as beautiful as Merina de Cordoba. But the warning of my old nurse rings true: I am like a sword that has been too highly tempered. The edge is keen, but*

*the blade snaps under strain. The day will come when my tormentors*
*call me what they have made me: "Juana La Loca, the Mad Queen."*

✠

Juan and I have a welcome guest at the Alcazar Palace in late
July, when Diego Columbus comes to stay with us. At the
river port of Seville, his father is securing a ship, the *Santa
Maria*, and buying supplies for his voyage. Two smaller ships,
the *Pinta* and the *Niña*, are being readied in the western ports
of Palos and Moguer.

The weather in Seville is hotter than I have ever known it.
A wax candle left in the sun dissolves into a greasy puddle in
minutes.

Week by week, throughout the summer, more Jewish
families depart the city, but most remain, silent and anxious,
in their Seville homes. It is as if they cannot grasp the enormity
of the calamity edging closer to them each day.

The final day, the deadline for the edict, arrives.

The previous night never cooled off; even at sunrise the
heat is oppressive.

Juan, Diego and I go for a swim in the Alcazar's reservoir.
This slim rectangular pool, inside a grotto-like tunnel, stays
cool even on the hottest days. The three of us wear light cotton
overshirts and trousers as we float in the water. Outside the
shaded grotto, the mid-morning sun is blinding white and
ripples of heat rise from the baking ground; the white doves
nesting in the palm trees coo sleepily.

I cup handfuls of cool water and pour it over my hair and
my face.

Then, I am the first to hear it: a deep, mournful sound, like a tidal wave surging against the walls of the Alcazar. It comes from the narrow warren of streets on the other side.

"What is it?" Juan asks, as I swim to the side and climb out of the pool.

Juan and Diego follow me, dripping water on the paving stones as we run toward the sound. A guard, high on the ramparts of the Alcazar wall, is watching something below him. We scramble up the narrow stone steps to join the soldier. The heat is so intense that our clothes are dry by the time we reach the top.

From our vantage point, we look through a mass of tumbling roses and jasmine, down into the tiny, twisting streets of the Juderia: the Jewish quarter.

The sound comes from people crowding the labyrinth of alleyways. I see bearded old men in skull caps and prayer shawls carrying the great, seven-branched, menorah candle holders; rabbis with torah scrolls rescued from synagogues soon to become churches and women clutching their precious books and their children.

"They are leaving Seville," Juan says flatly.

"I don't know why they waited so long," Diego says. "Today's the deadline."

Juan's eyes darken. "They cannot believe the decree ordering them out of Spain is true. They hoped that Mama and Papa would relent at the last minute – maybe let them stay if they paid higher taxes, or some sort of ransom. The Spanish kings are the protectors of the Jewish community."

The young guard standing next to us says, "The soldiers are going from house to house. The final warning. The Jews must be out of Seville by sunset, or baptised."

The houses of the Juderia snuggle against the Alcazar walls, as if to emphasise their special relationship with the Spanish royals inside the palace itself. Tomorrow, the Juderia will be re-named *Santa Cruz*, 'Holy Cross'.

I lean over the ramparts for a better view. In one group I see two brothers, richly dressed in the Jewish style, but wearing gold chains with crosses. They cling to a woman, who I assume is their sister. The young woman's husband holds the halter of a mule, panniers loaded with their belongings. The young couple are dressed for a journey, and her *converso* brothers are begging them to stay.

On the street corner, by the Church of Santa Maria – once a synagogue – a priest has set up a great silver baptismal font brimming with holy water. The priest brandishes a scallop shell from the shrine of Santiago de Compostela, dipping it into the holy water and offering to baptise, at the last minute, anyone wanting to stay in their homes.

I know that Don Isaac Abravanel lives in Seville, and I pray that the Abravanels have decided to convert. *Perhaps, even now, our trusted royal treasurer and his wife are back in Granada.*

Then, by a doorway further down the street, I see Doña Sara Abravanel being helped onto a riding mule by one of her sons. She is kissing the faces of her children, who have chosen to become *conversos* and stay behind.

I see Don Isaac, locking the front door to his house and taking the great bronze entry key to his home. He carefully wraps the key in a yellow silk handkerchief and tucks it securely into a pouch on his belt. He looks up and sees me. His sad eyes give no sign of acknowledgment.

"Is that the royal treasurer?" Diego asks.

I nod my head numbly, *yes*.

"I don't see why he's taking his house key with him," Diego says. "He won't need that anymore."

Juan turns toward him angrily. "He might."

"What do you mean?"

"Don Isaac is taking his key because he hopes, one day, to come back to Seville."

"Impossible. The edict says they are banned from Spain forever."

"Today, that is the law," Juan says softly. "But when I am king, I can change that law."

Diego's jaw drops and my eyes widen. "Careful what you say," I whisper. But the guard has heard my brother; he shifts his weight and tightens his grip on his halberd. He thinks, *Grand Inquisitor Torquemada pays well for this kind of information.*

"Let's leave," Juan says.

I cannot bear watching the scenes below us. We return to the garden. Diego says goodbye to us; he goes to assist his father at the docks and sail the *Santa Maria* to join the ships *Pinta* and the *Niña* at Palos harbour.

Juan and I sit on a bench in the garden. He reaches for his guitar and touches the strings in the melancholy rhythm of *cante jondo*. This is the music of mourning, of heartbreak, and it sears my soul.

"Juana, you must have seen, in the Seville cathedral, the words written on the tomb of our ancestor Fernando the Wise."

I nod. King Fernando *El Sabio's* epitaph is inscribed in three languages: Latin, Arabic and Hebrew.

"He is the King of the Three Religions. I promise you, that I will be the same."

"You will be Spain's best king, even better than Papa." *I admire my brother's courage and sense of justice, but at the same time I fear the deadly enemies who will oppose his ideas.*

✠

Our sorrow is temporarily pushed aside the next day, when the Duke of Medina Sidonia takes us on his promised hunting trip and we leave Seville, traveling into the Andalucian countryside with his extended family and entourage. We ride through the small traditional Christian villages, the *pueblos blancos*, that gleam in fresh coats of whitewash and are bright with ceramic pots of flowers. In each town, the Duke of Medina Sidonia introduces Don Juan, Prince of the Asturias, to the town leaders, the *Alcaldes*.

I watch with pride, standing next to and slightly behind my brother, as the *Alcaldes* from these Andalucian frontier towns step forward to swear allegiance to their prince, and to the new united Spain that our Trastamara family has forged in victory.

Towns are very important to the Spanish. For untold generations, Christian families crowded together in their tiny villages in the mountains, like nesting swallows under the eves of tall buildings. Rural townspeople depended on their neighbours for protection against a hostile world.

It is said that in Italy, a man is defined by his blood family. In Spain, a man – whether rich or poor – is defined by his *pueblo*. In a land at war for the 700 years of the Reconquista, the bonds of allegiance to one's *pueblo* are paramount.

Lord Sales explained to me that in northern countries, the great aristocratic landowners demand total obedience and subservience from the peasants who work for them. In Spain, no matter which noble family balances at the apex of the social pyramid, a man's *pueblo* is his security. Everyone knows that the most powerful man can be a rich warlord one day, and the next day, he is no more than bloated corpse on the battlefield, with vultures circling in the sky above to mark his passing.

Only the *pueblos* endure; clinging to the rocks, to the hilltops, surviving the crashing waves of time and fate, victories and defeats.

✠

From the sierras above Seville and Huelva, our hunting party makes its way down to the coast. In early August we reach the Duke's large hunting estate of Coto Doñana, on the wild Atlantic shore. The heat and mosquitos drive us to make camp at the beach at Matalascañas, where the cool sea breezes drive away the insects.

Tents are pitched next to the old Moorish coastal watchtower of Torre de Higuera. Wells of sweet water are dug in the sand, for the fresh water rises above the salt water table.

Fishermen bring their catch to sell to the royal party.

Just before sunset, while the servants prepare dinner at camp, Juan and I and the younger members of the duke's family ride down the beach to a second watchtower, called the Torre del Loro. We race to the tower and pull our horses up.

"We are close – just a few more hours riding time – to the Rio Tinto estuary and the harbour at Palos," says young Pablo Guzman, one of our host's sons.

Juan nods. "Where Columbus is readying his ships. He said he'd sail from Palos."

The sun edges lower, almost touching the horizon, and the evening wind rises. I shout when I see the sails of three caravels. "It's him! It must be him!" I shade my eyes with my hand.

We ride our horses into the surf until the waves lap the horses' bellies. I take off my hat and wave it at the ships.

There is no sign in response, for the sails are rapidly disappearing out to sea. "They are too far away to see us," I say dispiritedly.

The next day we ride to the Franciscan monastery at La Rabida, where Diego greets us. "My father and his ships left yesterday, at sunset, " he tells us.

"We saw them," I say, before we go into the chapel to pray for the *marineros* of Palos and Moguer, and Columbus.

The monks of La Rabida encouraged Columbus through the long dark years when he suffered bitter rejection after rejection for his plans; now, they are holding a vigil for the voyage of the *Niña*, the *Pinta*, and the *Santa Maria*.

The monastery is built on a promontory overlooking the sea, and Juan, Diego and I stand together outside the chapel.

Diego says, "I know that my father will find what he is searching for out there." He sweeps his hand toward the horizon, then gently touches my brother's arm. "And whatever he finds, Prince Juan, one day you will be king of it."

✠

Diego accompanies us on our journey back to Granada. We ride eastwards along the coast, visiting at the great seaport of Cadiz, where Juan wants to inspect the maritime defenses. Then we ride to Tarifa, Gibraltar and Algecerias; from these forts, we see across the straits, to the coast of the Islamic Kingdom of Morocco. If a counterattack from our enemies comes, it will be launched across this narrow stretch of water.

Juan and the Duke of Medina Sidonia approve the state of the defenses. We ride on, and the mood of the party grows more light-hearted. Every day is spent riding and hunting, either with falcons or greyhounds, *galgos*.

I love being with my brother, but there are subtle changes in our lives, for we are no longer children. Juan is now fourteen years old, and, in three months, I will be thirteen.

Hunting and riding each day with the Guzman family, we are a mixed group, but during the evenings in town, we divide. The young Guzman boy cousins, Diego and Juan go out on the town until the sun rises, while we females are cloistered indoors. The iron grilles of the town-house windows, the *rejas*, now separate us.

I find the Guzman girls convivial company. We sing and dance, while their family retainers play the guitar. The older women of the household join us and servants bring trays of drinks and food.

The girls are full of gossip, and we recline on large *almohadas*, cushions, as we talk until past midnight.

"Your brother, Prince Juan," fifteen-year-old Luisa de Guzman sighs. "He's so handsome! And so *simpatico!*"

I smile with pleasure when I hear Juan praised. This summer, he has grown taller and stronger, the sun bronzing his skin and streaking ruby lights into his dark hair.

"Everyone in Algecerias is wondering who the Prince will marry," Luisa giggles.

"Well, he hasn't mentioned anyone to me. He tells me everything."

One of the older women looks up from her needlework. "I've heard that Margaret Habsburg might be a possible bride for Prince Juan."

"Not her!" I roll my eyes heavenward. "That awful guardian of hers, Father Adrian, came to stay at court and we couldn't get rid of him. He probably started the engagement rumours himself."

"Father Adrian is a great friend of Inquisitor Torquemada," another sister whispers.

I shrug. "Well, he's gone now, and I hope he stays in the North, along with all the Habsburgs."

Luisa takes another sip of wine. "Of course, every family in Spain hopes Prince Juan will fall in love with one of their daughters." She rises from her cushion, does a graceful pirouette and comes to sit next to me. "And," she pauses dramatically, "it's said that the greatest man in Rome has hopes for his daughter and Prince Juan."

"What?" I demand, startled. This is news to me.

"Guess who she is?" Luisa counters. "She's your age."

I shake my head angrily, *no*.

"Lucrezia Borgia!" Luisa cries.

"Oh, surely not!" I jump up from the cushion. "Lucrezia's illegitimate. Mama would never allow it."

This piece of gossip worries me. The Spanish-Italian Borgia family are distantly related, through marriage, to the rulers of Aragon. Lucrezia's father, Cardinal Rodrigo Borgia, has just become pope, taking the title Pope Alexander VI. *A pope with two bastard sons and an illegitimate daughter. No, not a suitable match for Juan at all.*

"It's late, girls," the Duchess of Medina Sidonia says. "Off to bed, all of you." We kiss goodnight affectionately, and servants bring candles to light our way back to our rooms.

After the maid helps undress me and prepare my bed, I tell her to leave the lighted candle on the table. "I wish to read my book of devotions," I say.

When she leaves, I take the candle and tiptoe down the corridor. I stop by Juan's door and tap lightly. He's not back yet. *Again.*

Carefully shielding my candle from drafts, I enter his room. On the desk, weighted down under a small knife, is a letter. I put the candle down, slide the paper out from under the knife and open it. My heart stops as I read the lines.

It is written in Latin, in a schoolgirl hand. It begins by saying how much the writer hopes one day to meet the charming Spanish prince.

Then it continues.

My guardian, Father Adrian Boyens, has spoken highly of you, Prince Juan, and suggested I write to you. Father Adrian is sending your parents a portrait of me which I hope you will find pleasing.
With great affection,
Margaret Habsburg, Duchess of Burgundy

I tremble in rage. *How dare she? How dare that Habsburg girl write to my brother? Encouraged by Father Adrian, no doubt.*

I put down the letter and grip the knife. *If Adrian Boyens should come through the door at this moment, I would plunge the knife into his heart. He is an accursed shadow, I knew it from the first time I saw him, in the courtyard at Santa Fe. And now this! Margaret Habsburg? Even Lucrezia Borgia would be preferable as sister-in-law!*

I rip the letter to pieces and throw it on the floor, stamping furiously on the fragments. I turn and run out of the room, back to my own chamber and a sleepless night.

The next day, Juan confronts me about the letter. I remain defiant.

"Juana, you shouldn't be reading my letters," he says. "And why did you tear it to pieces?"

"I don't want you to write back to her."

"I'm sorry if you're jealous, but I'm not a child anymore. I am Prince of the Asturias." He reaches out and takes both my hands. "Mama and Papa have told me to start thinking about the possibility of finding a suitable bride. Since my illness, they worry about the succession. Marriage is my duty as their heir, but you will always be my most beloved sister. My twin."

I hug him closely; his words console me, but my antipathy against Margaret Habsburg grows.

The next night, when Juan is out with Diego and the Guzman brothers, I pray he might encounter, sitting modestly behind a *reja* festooned with red roses, a beautiful Spanish girl of a noble household and fall in love. *Perhaps he will choose*

*Luisa, the daughter of the Duke of Medina Sidonia? Any girl – any girl but Margaret Habsburg.*

✠

A week later, we take our leave of the Medina Sidonia family and Juan, Diego and I ride further east along the coast to Torremolinos. There we are re-united with our dear friend Lord Edmund Sales, back from his pilgrimage to Santiago de Compostela and settling in at his estate on the coast. Don Edmundo tells us that he enjoys being near the sea.

"In England the sea is cold and grey. Here the water is blue and warm," he says, laughing. He has just come back from wading in the surf and getting knocked down by a rogue wave. He looks like Neptune emerging from the water.

I am pleased that Don Edmundo will accompany us back to Granada. We will travel through the Alpujarra mountains to get there.

"Queen Isabel encouraged me to write to the Condesa de Moya," he says, his eyes brightening. "So I did. Doña Beatriz is much better and wrote back that she hopes to see me."

I clap my hands with joy. This is an exchange of love letters that I heartily approve of. "I'm so pleased! Tia Beatriz cares for you, I know she always has."

Don Edmundo beams.

Our route back to Granada leads through a series of precipitous passes in the high mountains. Don Edmundo points out the mountain towers guarding the frontier of Boabdil's new domain.

"Your father was wise to give him this place as his own little kingdom. If the Moors had retreated, fighting, to these mountains and caves, we would still be at war."

I look down at the twisting pewter ribbon of river below us. Above us are higher rocky slopes, and villages with crooked, narrow, goat tracks leading to them. Don Edmundo orders us to turn aside at the watchtower that marks the boundary leading to Boabdil's village. "His lands are protected by the peace treaty; we may not enter without his permission."

I think of Fatima living in that mountain village after her life in the Alhambra, feeling both pity and sorrow. Also fear; fear of the curse she wished upon me: *"May your own son one day destroy you, as my son has destroyed me. You will grow old and die, as I am condemned to die, in some poor, cold, miserable mountain village, sold out by those you trusted, betrayed by your own son."*

Then Juan strikes up a song, Don Edmundo and Diego join in, and I let go of my fear of the future; rejoicing in company of those I love.

Approaching the city of Granada, the weather is cooler. The leaves of the birch trees are just beginning to turn the colour of translucent gold. When we reach the Alhambra Palace, our mother comes rushing out to meet us, with Isabella, Maria and Catalina close behind. Our father appears from the second courtyard.

It strikes me how my parents have aged in the three months we have been away. It is as if the will to conquer Granada has kept them going for so long and now, with victory, all the infirmities that they held fiercely at bay have swept in to claim them. The lines on their faces are cut deeper.

161

My mother's blonde hair is threaded with silver; there is a slight stoop to her proud walk and a thickening of her once lithe figure. The grey hair at my father's temples is more pronounced. Papa has begun to limp slightly on his right leg, from an old wound.

Isabella looks thinner than ever. Maria and Catalina have adapted happily to life in the Alhambra, cosseted as any odalisques in the harem.

My parents exclaim at how Juan and I have grown and changed. "The *camino*, the open road, teaches you how to live, *querida*," Papa says to me, kissing me in welcome.

I have learned a great lesson in life: how to follow my own *camino*, my own road. Many of Juan's songs and the songs of the Spanish troubadours tell of love and fate; even more sing of *El Camino*. For seven centuries, we Spanish have been a restless people living in our saddles, as mobile as desert Bedouins. We moved with our armies and our horses and our families, pushing south in the *Reconquista*.

Life is always a journey. Life is a pilgrimage. Life is the road to Granada.

*For me, that summer of traveling the camino with my beloved brother Juan was not the end. Like the ships of Columbus, my life's journey was just beginning.*

✠

The night of our return, before supper, my mother declares that she and her daughters will take over the women's section of the Moorish baths. I am grateful for the luxury after the long, dusty ride. I find it delicious, floating in the warm, perfumed water with the Moorish maidservants washing my hair. Later, I lay on a marble table for a massage. The baths are softly lit by pierced lanterns that throw flickering shadows on the golden stone walls. The air is fragrant with incense. King Fernando, Juan, Lord Sales, and the Aragonese courtiers use the men's baths.

Afterward, we attend mass and go to supper. I see the missing places at the tables, yet neither of my parents speak of it; no one speaks of it. The Edict of Expulsion is not discussed in front of my parents. Don Isaac Abravanel is gone, as is Doctor Badoc. The new royal treasurer is Don Abraham Seneor. He is a newly-baptised *converso*. I am relieved to see Moises Sanchez, the royal falconer; he has changed his name to Manuel on his baptism.

I watch my sisters at supper and my heart aches for the Jewish families divided; Jewish brothers and sisters who stayed in Spain, as their siblings went into exile.

The same fate may be ours, as royal children. Juan, the heir, will stay in Spain when he marries. *Hopefully*, I pray, *the woman he marries will not be Margaret Habsburg. Or Lucrezia Borgia.*

Margaret's portrait, painted by a Flemish artist, arrives at the Alhambra. It is a new Northern style of painting – with the finest of tiny brushstrokes capturing colour and light – but I can't see how it flatters Margaret. Her eyebrows and eyelashes are so pale that they appear non-existent, with slightly bulging blue eyes and a prominent square jawline. Her elaborate box-like Northern headdress crushes her hair.

"She looks like a fish to me," I sniff. "Margaret Fishface of Burgundy."

Juan shrugs. "You can't judge someone's soul by one portrait."

Our mother is enchanted with this new Flemish style of painting and she writes to Father Adrian to send an artist from Flanders to Granada to paint portraits of her own daughters.

*I wonder how this Flemish artist will portray us? If some foreign prince likes our faces, where will we be sent?* Isabella is promised to the Portuguese King: not far for her to travel, Portugal joins Castile's western border. Baby sister Catalina is Princess of Wales, destined for England when she grows up. That is much further, and a long sea voyage for her. Shy, pretty, home-loving Maria. *Surely, my parents will not marry her to the Archduke of Burgundy, and send her so far away?* I suspect that my parents will try to find an Iberian aristocrat for her to marry, to keep her in Spain.

*And me. I want to stay in Granada forever, and no one has contradicted my plan to become a Franciscan nun. The convent is within the walls of the Alhambra.*

✠

I long for my family to remain united and happy, but fault lines appear, like hairline cracks in a fine glazed vase. My parents are quarreling more, disagreements simmering with a fierce undercurrent of mutual resentment. I learn that my father is a womaniser and has always had mistresses. When we were younger, our mother tried to keep the knowledge of these women from us. Each time she discovered a new mistress, the queen was quick to marry her off to some nobleman living in a distant corner of Spain, far from the royal court. Although

Fernando's infidelity hurt her deeply, Isabel never stopped loving him.

In his own way, Fernando loves Isabel above all the women in his life. He is a devoted father who adores his children; he even loves the illegitimate ones, whose existence I learn about for the first time. He no longer makes the effort to be discreet.

Each day the friction increases between my parents. I see my mother's tight-lipped face, I hear my father making excuses to ride into the city of Granada in the evenings. Their arguments over Columbus and his voyage acquire a cutting edge. "Can you wear your 'Necklace of the Twelve Cameos' to mass?" my father asks. "It's always suited you so well."

"Perhaps I'll wear my pearls instead."

"I haven't seen the cameo necklace for months now."

She makes a fluttering movement of her hand in dismissal.

He frowns. "I suppose your necklace went to pay for that man's ships?"

"The ships will return. My investment will pay off."

"They might, or they might not, but at least Juan will inherit all of my Kingdom of Aragon. I would never risk his inheritance for a dream of sailing – *sailing* – into oblivion." He repeats the word with the scorn of the land-based commander.

"Never mind, my darling. The India spice trade will pay back double, triple, the money raised by my jewels." She thinks, but does not mention, the prophecy: *the King of Spain who will take the cross to worlds as yet unknown. Our son, Prince Juan.*

My brother and I exchange embarrassed glances. Poor

Diego Columbus. We all wonder what has happened to his father; the ships have been gone for four long months.

*There is no way we could have known, in early October, as the birch trees scattered their golden leaves over the gardens of the Alhambra, that Columbus planted the flag of Castile on the shores of a New World across the Atlantic Ocean.*

✠

Juan is the bulwark that my parents depend on to guard against their greatest fears.

My father's fear is of betrayal. There was a horror of *renegados*, renegades, during the Granada War. *Renegados* were men who renounced their Christian faith and became Muslim. Whenever the Christian army captured these renegade fighters in battle, they were given the chance to return to their Christian roots, or die as the Muslim converts they had become. These *renegados*, obsessed and suicidal warriors, were a torment to my father. Here were men who had deserted their families, their king and their faith. He fears that without a strong Christian military leader, weak men will drift into other alliances.

For my mother, her fear is civil war. In the past, our Trastamara family was split between legitimate heirs to the throne and ambitious royal bastards raising armies of their own. Her husband's mistresses are more than a source of personal heartache; Isabel knows that mistresses produce illegitimate part-royal babies, who grow up to jealous and dangerous adulthood.

The threat of civil war in Spain rumbles and smokes like

a sleeping dragon beneath the feet of our Trastamara family. The queen knows that civil war means that the country that she and her husband have hammered together will tear itself apart in an orgy of self-destruction.

Prince Juan is their hope. Prince Juan is the future of a united and prosperous Spain. Prince Juan is the fulfillment of the Granada Prophecy. As the law of Spain now stands, only Juan can inherit both the Kingdom of Aragon and the Kingdom of Castile. Fernando's Kingdom of Aragon has, in the past, restricted inheritance to royal men. My father is confident that he can convince his nobles to change this law to include his daughters in the succession, but he has not yet done so.

The Kingdom of Castile can be ruled either by a man or a woman; and my sisters and I are heirs of Queen Isabel's crown.

*Only, please God, the Queen prays, keep my only son safe and well to inherit my kingdom.*

✠

The Feast of the Epiphany, January 6th, 1493, is first anniversary of our triumphant entry into Granada; as a family, we go to Mass and Holy Communion. I kneel in the royal chapel – once the Alhambra's mosque – and while the nuns chant the litany, I watch the clouds of incense swirling up to the ceiling, brushing the Moorish calligraphy of the Koran.

My parents kneel side by side. I know they have changed their wills regarding where they will be buried. With all their great cities of Spain to chose from, Isabel and Fernando have decided that their final resting place will be here, in Granada.

My lace *mantilla* slips to my shoulders and I pull it back to cover my hair. *I shiver with premonition, seeing a vision of their carved effigies, lying on high marble plinths.*

After Mass, our family, with Lord Sales, Father Cisneros, our guests, priests and the abbess of the Franciscan covent, retire to the Courtyard of the Ambassadors. The braziers burn fragrant wood and platters of food are handed around. Hundreds of tiny Moorish lamps, of coloured glass, are carefully lit. Overhead, the sky fills with stars. Everyone is talking and laughing and singing. *A year in Granada!*

Lord Sales is seated next to Doña Beatriz, her scarred face and black eyepatch softened under the gossamer-thin silk veil she wears, secured by a tortoiseshell comb. She is at ease in his devoted company. Juan is happy and leading the songs, as the servants bring out more platters of food and pour more wine.

I sip my wine and look at Diego Columbus, who tries bravely to smile back at me. He clasps his goblet with nails that are bitten to the quick, no doubt thinking of his father. We have still heard nothing of the ships that sailed from Palos in August.

I sit next to my sister Maria; her little dog Chica is curled in her lap, eating tidbits from her fingers. One of the Moorish servants winces as she replenishes Maria's plate. I whisper to my sister, "I don't think she likes dogs anymore than she likes pigs." We giggle.

We listen to a new song Juan has composed, then he calls on me to dance for the guests. The musicians follow Juan's lead, and the guitar and mandolin and tambourines begin a flamenco rhythm. I step out into the center of the circle of musicians and lose myself in the music. I hear the *palmas*, the rhythmic clapping of hands in time to the music, and I swirl in the graceful movements of the dance that are as natural to me as breathing.

There are shouts of encouragement and approval from the guests. I finish with a bow and everyone applauds. I hear my father say to Lord Sales, "Juana is the best dancer in Granada. My beautiful daughter has many gifts, but the greatest is her dancing." Warm and out of breath, I go over to my mother and kiss her cheek. "I'll be back in a minute," I murmur. She nods, assuming I am leaving for a call of nature.

But no; my need is to be away from the happy, talkative *fiesta*. I walk down the dark corridors again, reminded of the night I encountered Fatima. I wonder where the haughty, aristocratic old woman is this evening. I wonder if she even pretends to celebrate the Moorish festival of Eid, gathered with her few remaining ladies in their goatherd village high in the Alpujarras.

I love walking though the Alhambra, where buildings open into gardens and fountains, then flow back into the rooms. The perimeter wall of the palace hugs the heights of the cliff called La Sabika. I find a place where the stone wall lowers into a broad, flat surface, a *mirador*, to view the city. I pull my cloak about me and climb to sit on the honey-coloured stone, which feels as comfortable and yielding as a pillow.

I know how a falcon must feel, settling on the familiar glove of its owner. I dangle my slippered feet over the edge of the wall, looking at the lights from the houses of the Albaicin quarter opposite. The Albaicin and the Alhambra face each other on two steep hills. The view from one is of the other, like the houses across the narrow streets of Seville, each looking into the other's windows.

I can see pale lights behind the barred windows of a new monastery, the Monastery of San Nicolas. *Do they look out tonight at us, I wonder, and remember the centuries the Moors spent in these gardens?*

I play with a tassel on my belt and look up at the stars. The court gossips are now certain that my sister Maria will be betrothed to the young Archduke of Burgundy, Phillipe Habsburg, as arranged by Adrian Boyens. *Poor Maria, let her go North, taking my prayers with her.*

I never want to leave Granada. Becoming a nun in the Alhambra's Franciscan convent is better than being sent away to the alien Northern court of Flanders, and the arms of some Habsburg archduke.

I know that my spirit will never be at peace anywhere but here. I will never leave Granada, I vow. Even if they send me away, I will somehow find my way back.

I run my fingers over the flat stone where I sit. I dream that my breath will turn into golden-coloured stones and cool marble pillars, flowering trees, with the fragrance of lemons and roses. *And perhaps*, I think, *sometime ages from now, someone will see a girl, a shadow of a girl in a blue gown, sitting by a fountain pool, her fingertips rippling the mirror surface of the water.*

What if Papa won't let me become a nun? What if I really, truly, must marry someone? *Well, if I must marry, then I will bring my bridegroom here. He will walk in these gardens with me and kiss me softly.* I touch my fingertips to my lips and close my eyes.

I hear a footstep behind me. "Juana, what are you doing

here? It's cold, you must be freezing." It is Lord Sales. "Doña Beatriz is worried about you, she sent me to find you."

He puts his hands on my waist and lifts me down from the wall. "You are quite the wanderer, aren't you? Come with me."

He holds out his hand and I take it. His fingers are warm and strong; a warrior's hand with a gentle touch. I feel safe with him.

We walk back together toward the lights of the Hall of the Ambassadors, to the music and laughter that drifts on the night wind in the gardens of the Alhambra.

# PART II
# Sailing North

Winter passes into spring and with the return of the swallows to the Alhambra, comes the news. Christopher Columbus – Admiral of the Ocean Sea – is back safely from his great Atlantic voyage. He makes his return landfall on the western coast and couriers ride in fast relays to Granada, to tell the queen and king. Diego Columbus is jubilant, for his father is alive and his dream vindicated.

I join my parents, Juan and my sisters for the admiral's reception. Columbus bows before my mother. He orders his bearers to bring in small wooden chests, filled with his discoveries: unusual trinkets of gold jewellery and exotic dried fruits and seeds. There are a dozen parrots of brilliant hues, four tiny monkeys with brilliant orange fur and six native people of the West, whom he called 'Indians'.

I look anxiously at my father. He sits stonily on his throne and drums his fingers on the armrest. "Is this all there is?" he asks the admiral. "I don't see much gold. If you went to India, where are the bales of silk and the chests of spices?"

My mother blushes at his rudeness, taps my father's arm and whispers to him, "The admiral told me that these small gifts are from the outlying islands he reached; the silks and spices and more gold will be found on the mainland of India."

My father stares at Columbus. "Then why didn't you keep going to the mainland of India?"

"My Lord." Columbus bows. "Our ships were caught in a storm at the islands; the *Santa Maria* was wrecked."

"We are extraordinarily grateful for the *Niña* and the *Pinta*, the ships from Palos and Moguer, which brought you safely home," my mother beams. "And grateful to the Pinzon cousins, of those towns, who captained them." She is obviously enchanted with the objects laid before her as proof of his discovery.

The admiral bows again. "If you see fit to give me more ships and more men, I will sail back and reach the mainland." His hand is over his heart and his eyes are filled with wordless longing. *Will there be money for another voyage?* He looks hopefully from the queen to the king.

My father's eyes, calculating values, go from the Indians to the marmosets to the parrots. The largest bird, with its extravagant gold and blue feathers, squawks loudly on its perch. Papa crosses his arms and frowns.

Mama ignores his bad temper and turns to Juan. *Another voyage?* She inclines her head wordlessly.

Juan nods, *yes*.

Isabel draws a deep breath. "Admiral, the Kingdom of Castile will support you. Prepare another voyage to these lands you have found." The queen studies the six natives, standing in a silent group. She stands and beckons them to approach her. Their chaplain, a young priest who learned their language, encourages them to kneel before the queen.

I am transfixed by these strangers from the far side of the sea.

Columbus says, apologetically, that he had captured twenty-five of these Indians to bring to Spain, but most died on the voyage. Only these six have survived. *What I sense, wordlessly, in their manner, is an inner strength beyond measure.*

I have seen Moors and the dark Africans; I have seen the Christians of farthest northern Europe with the palest of blue eyes and white-blond hair. I have even seen a Chinese, a servant sent by the Portuguese king as a diplomatic gift to my sister Isabella. But these four young men and two women are different. They have copper-coloured skins, and their long, glossy hair is braided with small white shells and brilliant parrot feathers. Their chaplain has dressed them for court in Moorish-stye robes and they hold themselves proudly.

The priest tells us, "In their home islands, they wear little clothing, but they are pleased to adapt to our customs here. I have learned that they are pagans – neither Jew nor Moor nor Christian. Some tribes worshiped images and others worshipped the sun or the wind. They have now been baptised."

He pauses, then steps forward and hands my mother six small crosses on gold chains. "During the voyage home, I carved these crosses while I instructed *los indios* in the true faith. My Lady, would you please present them with these crosses and agree to be their godmother?"

My mother smiles radiantly. Each small cross is carved from a strange new type of reddish-colored wood. She carefully places a gold chain around each neck, resting her hand in blessing on each head. Then she asks them to stand before her. She looks into their dark eyes, her own grey-blue eyes shining with tears of emotion.

"You who accept the faith of our Lord Jesus Christ are my brothers and sisters," she says to each one.

My father mutters under his breath, "Brothers and sisters in Christ. Not even any profit selling them as slaves, then."

"Of course not," my mother retorts, as she returns to sit beside him on the dais. "Only pagans might be bought and sold as slaves. The law of Castile forbids the enslavement any Christian – no matter what their race."

I look at Juan. Whatever our mother's faults and failings, we know her horror of slavery. We witnessed her fury when she freed the Christian slaves at Malaga.

I smile tentatively at the exotic strangers. Maria slips closer to pet the tiny monkeys, called marmosets by their keeper.

The *indios* become part of our royal court: the two young native women become my personal servants. They choose the Christian names Ana and Teresa, and in time they will become my most trusted friends and confidants.

Columbus makes a grateful salute to my mother and Juan, then departs. In September, 1493, he sails from Spain with seventeen ships. This time, Diego Columbus accompanies his father.

✠

On my fourteenth birthday, November 6th, 1493, my father suggests that he and I ride together, just the two of us, from the Alhambra to oversee the olive harvest. I adore these rare times alone with my father. We ride to a small hill, overlooking the plains, where acres of olive trees planted in orderly rows. The Moorish workers are busy harvesting the olives to be processed into oil; the harvest is a festive event, with entire families – grandparents, teenagers, even toddlers – helping out.

We stop our horses under one of the trees. I have always felt that olive trees are talismans of good fortune, their gnarled ancient trunks standing sentinel over the land.

My father reaches out and touches one of the branches. "This tree is 2000 years old. The Romans planted it when they first came to Spain. It was here before the Arabs came and it's still here now that they've gone. It will – God willing – still be here 500 years from now. Still giving olives to process for eating, or to make olive oil."

I nod in agreement.

"You know, Juana, you have always been the wisest of my daughters, as well as the most beautiful."

I blush and stroke my horse's mane.

"Our family is like an olive tree. The Trastamaras: our roots are in Spain, deep in the soil, surviving droughts and floods and war." He looks at me. "I need your help, Juana."

I stare back at him, surprised. "Why, Papa, of course. I'd do anything for you."

"We have won Granada. For twelve years of the war, I put the needs of my own Kingdom of Aragon to the side, to help your mother. Granada is now part of her Kingdom of Castile."

"Yes, Papa."

"We made an agreement, your mother and I. I would help her win Granada and in return she would help me in my war against the King of France. I'll be leaving soon, for Barcelona. There I will raise my army among the Catalans of Aragon. Juan will be coming with me."

My heart tightens. The two men I love most in my life going off to war.

My father clears his throat before continuing. "The Kingdom of France is a powerful and envious neighbour on my northern border. The French king covets my lands in Spain and my dominions in Italy. I need allies."

"Of course, Papa. Will the English help?"

"The English like nothing better than fighting the French, they are old foes, but I need even more help."

My heart sinks, and I can barely raise a whisper. "The Habsburgs?"

"I'm asking you to please help me. The Emperor Maximilian is keen for a marriage alliance with us."

For two years now, ever since Father Adrian returned to the North, marriage rumours swirled about court. My parents refused to confirm anything.

"Juan will marry Margaret of Burgundy?" I ask.

"Yes." He pauses for a long time, studying the silvery branches of the olive tree. "But they want more. Juana, I know you said you wanted to become a nun, but I have never thought that a very suitable future for you. Could you put that idea to one side, just for me? Could you consider marrying the Archduke of Burgundy?"

I feel the blood drain from my face, and hear a sound like ocean waves pounding in my ears.

"What about Maria? I thought that Maria would marry Archduke Phillipe?" I say frantically. I feel as if I might faint and cling with both hands to the pommel of my saddle for support.

My father sighs and snaps a small twig, heavy with ripe olives, off the bough. "I'll be honest with you: Maria was the first choice of the Habsburgs, but your mother said no." There is a flatness in his voice. "She said that you must be the daughter to leave."

His words stun me. *What have I done, that my mother wants me to leave? Does my father realise what he is asking me to do? Leaving Spain may kill me. Am I strong enough to do this? An olive tree is strong, but could it be uprooted and exiled to a cold, alien land?*

"I don't need your answer right now," he says hurriedly. "Just think about it, please. Trust me. Juan's betrothal is settled, but the emperor is pushing for a second marriage with our family. I would only negotiate for your engagement; a wedding might never happen. The final decision will be yours." Papa leans over in his saddle, and kisses me.

In silence, we gather our reins and ride back through the olive grove to the Alhambra, leaving behind us the chatter and singing of the families harvesting the crop in the late afternoon sunlight.

✠

I am growing from a girl into a young woman. No longer will I be able to roam freely about the Alhambra and the City of Granada, but must be accompanied by a *duenna*. Every smile at a young man is noted and commented on.

I turn to my beloved Tia Beatriz. "I've talked to Juan about this proposal," I say, breathing in the fragrance of a red rose in condesa's courtyard garden. "He says to accept it. He marries the sister and, if I chose, I marry the brother. Juan and I will remain 'the twins' as always."

"It will be a great honour to become the Archduchess of Burgundy," Doña Beatriz says soothingly.

"I wish that honour went to Maria. Going to Flanders means a long sea voyage. I've never been on the Atlantic Ocean. I would prefer to ride all the way north to Flanders, but we can't go across France because of Papa's war."

"When you go, I'll sail with you. So will Don Edmundo."

"Would you? It would mean so much to me." I bite my lip.

"I don't know what I'm more afraid of, the sea voyage or marrying Phillipe, or having to see that horrible Father Adrian."

"He's no longer Father Adrian. He is now Bishop Adrian, Bishop of Antwerp," Doña Beatriz says dryly. She thinks to herself, *no doubt Adrian Boyens is enthroned as bishop as a reward for securing this marriage alliance. The royal chaplain has risen, too. Father Cisneros is now Archbishop of Toledo, the highest church office in Spain. And the Inquisition grows more powerful each passing year. My poor Juana, what a world is being made for you. Will Lord Sales and I be strong enough to protect you?*

✠

As he readies for war against the King of France, my father grows more restless and bad tempered. In spite of the gold of Granada and the efficient tax-gathering of the new royal treasurer Don Abraham Seneor, Fernando chaffs bitterly at what he perceives to be his wife's divided loyalties. He feels that Queen Isabel would empty the treasury of Castile for Columbus' sailing ventures, but hold back money that Fernando needs in his war against the French king.

The war against the French is successful on the battlefield and the French King is defeated. The Kingdom of Aragon's frontier at the Pyrenees is safe and my father's dominions in Italy are secure. I am proud to welcome my father and brother back from the war. Juan is Prince of the Asturias in more than title, for he is now a warrior prince in the greatest tradition of Trastamaras.

The success of the Kingdom of Aragon in Europe is paralleled by the success of the Kingdom of Castile in the New World. In 1494, Queen Isabel signs the Treaty of Tordesillas with the other great Atlantic sailing nation, our neighbor Portugal, dividing the entire globe between these two Iberian maritime powers. The dividing line was drawn by Pope Alexander VI, Rodrigo Borgia.

In Seville, a small community of German printers arrive and begin producing books, with the support and encouragement of Queen Isabel and Prince Juan. *Los Alemanes*, 'the Germans', they are called, and everything rolls off their presses: Spanish manuscripts from the collections of the Moors, transcribed scrolls from antiquity and diaries and maps from the New World discoveries. *Los Alemanes* live and work in the district adjacent to the cathedral. In an ironic twist, the printing workshops are on one side of Seville's Guadalquivir river, disseminating revolutionary knowledge, while on the opposite bank of the river, the headquarters of the Inquisition in Castelo San Jorge ponders the impact.

Much to my brother Juan's regret, the great Flemish philosopher Erasmus never came to Spain. He chose, instead, to go to England.

✠

The summer of 1496, when I am sixteen and Juan seventeen, the arrangements are finalised for a double royal wedding. I will sail with an armada of Spanish ships to Flanders to marry the Archduke of Burgundy. Then the fleet will return home, bringing Margaret to marry Juan in Spain.

In my chamber off the Courtyard of the Two Sisters, I try on my wedding dress before it is packed for the voyage. My two maids, Teresa and Ana, help me dress; they will come with me to Flanders. My mother and Tia Beatriz stand by my side looking at the mirrored reflection. I see myself: dark auburn curls held back from my face by my jewelled headdress, my high-necked silk velvet gown, sumptuously embroidered with borders, in raised gold thread, of castles, lions, pomegranates and arrow sheaves. My dark, wide-set eyes, under thick eyebrows, stare back at me from the mirror. My slim fingers smooth the fabric of my skirt.

"You are too thin," Ana grumbles, as she takes in the back of the dress while holding pins in her mouth.

"I can't eat when I'm upset." I reply. *I'm beginning to sound like Isabella.*

"There's no reason for you to be upset," my mother says sharply. "You are going to marry the most eligible young man in Christendom."

I see Tia Beatriz look at my mother and then sadly back to me. She knows, as I do not, that Spanish spies at the Court of Burgundy report that Phillipe's primary interests are women – especially women – and the sport of jousting, and the latest fashions in clothing. He is easily bored, refuses to read books and considers statecraft to be the duty of his advisor, Bishop Adrian.

✠

Before we leave to ride to the port of Laredo in the far north of Spain, the royal court holds a farewell celebration for me in Granada.

After the feast, our family and courtiers ride to the plains beyond the city for a *corrida de toros*, or what Lord Sales calls a 'bullfight'. We encounter a big herd of the black wild cattle, the *toros bravos*, grazing in a flat valley, enclosed by steep hills.

On our approach, the cows and their calves gallop away into the hills. Staying to challenge us are the most powerful bulls.

The most daring riders compete against each other in *derribo y acosta*, running their horses alongside a beast and knocking it off its feet by a clever punch of the lance on its shoulder, timed to a critical moment of movement. This is a rough and tumble sport and we ladies, while mounted and armed with *garrochas*, long lances, in case of a charge, do not participate.

Juan and my father run their horses together as a team toward a bull, avoiding its slashing horns. Juan balances his *garrocha* strike perfectly and the bull tumbles to the ground.

Other officers and nobles also have their sons with them at the *corrida*. Don Pedro Cortes, from Extremadura, is accompanied by his son Hernando, a brash fourteen-year-old.

Young Hernando Cortes is dashing and a show-off, obviously trying to impress me and my sisters. We gather our horses around our mother's mount and watch the men who face the charge of the bulls. I see Hernando run his nervous horse toward an aggressive bull, which hooks a horn into his horse's side. The horse tumbles down, fatally wounded. Hernando manages to roll clear of the falling horse and, as he lies on the ground, the bull swerves toward him.

Five soldiers immediately jump from their horses and run on foot to the rescue, using their riding capes to draw the bull away. The furious bull continues snorting, pawing the earth, momentarily distracted. Another rider gallops up and stabs the bull's powerful withers with a sharpened lance.

Hernando scrambles to his feet, dusts himself off and angrily grabs a sword from one of the soldiers.

My mother watches, noticing everything. She turns to me. "You see how these men fight the bulls. From this, you can foretell their courage in battle."

Then the bull charges toward us and we spur our horses out of the way; I grip my *garrocha* ready for the bull's charge. Hernando runs between us to intercept the enraged beast, and it pauses to face him. Blood runs down the bull's muscled withers as it bellows and blows, pawing up great chunks of powdery earth in fury.

Hernando stands his ground, shouting a challenge to the animal, the two of them join in an intimate dance of death. The bull lowers its head to charge and Hernando rises over its neck, thrusting the sword between the shoulder blades, fully up the hilt, while nimbly avoiding the horns. The bull stops, as if turned to stone. Hernando holds up his hand in front of the bull's muzzle, which drips with bloody froth.

The bull exhales and collapses in death, its legs folding

beneath the body, the head outstretched at Hernando's boots. The soldiers rush to congratulate him.

Hernando cuts off the bull's ear as a trophy and brings it over to me. He looks into my eyes, his face dusty, a smear of blood down one cheek; his smile is cocksure and confident. I lean down from my saddle and accept the trophy.

My mother smiles at him approvingly. "You are fearless, young Hernando Cortes. We will need men like you in the New World."

*My mother's belief in prophecies will be fulfilled by this brash teenager. When he grows to manhood, Conquistador Commander Hernando Cortez will conquer Mexico in the name of his sovereign, the Queen of Spain. That queen will be me.*

✠

Juan kisses me goodbye before I board my ship at the port of Laredo. "My twin," he says affectionately. "I'll always be with you. Your new husband must treat you well, or he'll have to answer to me." He gives me his parting gift, which he had specially commissioned for me: an exquisite small 'Book of Hours', a prayer book. It is a traditional illuminated vellum manuscript, the calligraphy and paintings hand-made by the Franciscan nuns in their Alhambra convent. He has written both our names, and 'August 1496' on the inside cover. I will always keep this prayer book by my side; my library of other books, both manuscripts and the new printed books, will be safely packed in chests in the hold.

I look into my brother's eyes, a mirrored reflection of my own. We need no further words; we are like two halves of the same olive tree. Over the last few years, with our adolescence, we have spent more time apart; but the spiritual ties between us are stronger than ever.

Then I kiss my father farewell. I am overcome by a sense of déja-vu and I remember hugging him goodbye when he rode off to war at Granada. "I love you, Papa," I say. "This time, I will be the one who promises to return." He is unable to speak.

My mother and sisters help me arrange my things in my cabin on board, then my family leaves the ship and returns to shore. There are a hundred ships with an entourage of nearly 12,000 nobles, sailors, soldiers, clerics, and servants who will escort me to Flanders.

Lord Edmund Sales and Doña Beatriz, Condesa de Moya, accompany me in the flagship on the voyage north. The ships hoist sail and surge into the Bay of Biscay. I stand at the rail in the salt spray, watching the coast of Spain until it disappears from view. *Leaving home just before my seventeenth birthday; I now know the same knife-cutting pain all exiles feel.*

I am apprehensive about my first sea voyage, alert to the nightmare I had as a child about the battle on the warship.

But my servants Ana and Teresa show no sign of fear: they have sailed across the Atlantic with Columbus. Their matter-of-fact stoicism encourages me to be the same. Fortunately, I never get seasick on the voyage, though many others do. Lord Sales is pleased that I am not frightened, but exhilarated by the wind and waves. His plan, Lord Sales tells me, is to take me to Flanders, then he and Tia Beatriz will visit his estate in England before they return to Spain.

On board the ships are several families of *conversos*, whose ultimate destination is England. King Henry Tudor has announced that he is rescinding the centuries-old ban on Jews in England, and Sephardic exiles will be welcomed in his kingdom. Already, the Sultan of Turkey has encouraged a large community of Sephardic Jews to settle in Constantinople; when the Edict of Expulsion was decreed in Spain, the sultan sent ships to collect the Jewish refugees. In Turkey, the Sephardic community continues to use the language, customs and food of their Spanish homeland.

What Lord Sales and Tia Beatriz do not know, and what I struggle to conceal from them, is my terrible homesickness. In my mind, I return again to memories of the gardens of the Alhambra, to block out the towering waves and heaving ship and howling winds.

Our armada has been at sea for over six weeks when we reach the English Channel in late September. The weather so far has been reasonably consistent, but as we tack into the Channel for our final approach to the coast of Flanders, a great storm boils across the horizon.

Lord Sales takes control, telling the captain, "Find a harbour immediately. We're closer to England than Flanders at this point, let's take refuge quickly, before this storm gets worse."

The once-orderly procession of armada ships are scattered by the winds.

Through driving rain, darkness descends. Our captain sees a faint light – a lighthouse – on the English coast.

✠

Just before our ship struggles into the harbour, the main mast is toppled in the wind, dragging the rigging and sails into the water. We drop two anchors to hold the ship steady, and English fishermen, carrying lanterns, brave the storm to row to our rescue in their smaller boats.

"Where are we?" I gasp, as Lord Sales helps me clamber into an English fishing dingy. I clutch my new prayer book, wrapped in an oilskin, under my cloak. Ana and Teresa carry my jewel boxes. Other fishermen reach for Tia Beatriz, helping her to safety.

"We are near Portsmouth, this man tells me," Lord Sales shouts over the noise of the wind. Our Spanish captain, wet and frightened, says we cannot continue to Flanders until the ship is repaired. *It might take days, it might take weeks*, he says, wringing his hands. Tia Beatriz sensibly insists we get to shelter immediately and discuss the ship later.

Our rescuers lead us to an inn, perched on a hill overlooking the storm-swept shore. It is dark, with low, heavy beams that I have to duck under. The room is filled with smoke from a huge open fireplace.

The innkeeper puts more logs on the fire, and rushes to serve us, his unexpected guests, with flagons of ale and platters of bread and cheese. I take a sip of the ale, longing to get warm and dry. Tia Beatriz pulls a rough, three-legged stool over, and I collapse on it gratefully. Ana and Teresa help me out of my soaked outer garments, all thoughts of modesty banished in the emergency. Tia Beatriz hangs the clothes to dry before the fire. Ana takes charge of my precious prayer book, placing it with the jewel boxes which she and Teresa guard.

I sit near the fireplace in my undershift, a borrowed shawl

from the innkeeper's wife slipping down over my shoulders. I run my fingers through my wet hair, long auburn curls reflecting the light from the flames. I bend from my waist, closer to the fire, shaking my hair out vigorously, when a stranger strides into the crowded room. Everyone goes silent and makes way for him.

I look up at him through the cascade of my hair. I see him stop immediately, staring at me in surprise and wonder. The man is tall and wiry, perhaps almost as old as my father, with a hard, chiseled face, expressive eyes and a thin, aquiline nose.

Lord Sales turns around and his eyes widen. "My Lord! I did not know you were here." He rushes forward and drops to one knee before him.

The man puts a hand on Lord Sales' shoulder and bids him rise. "Edmund, my old friend. It's *your* arrival in England that is the surprise." The stranger begins pulling off his wet gloves. "I was hunting here in Hampshire, when the storm broke."

I stand up and face the man, tossing my hair back from my face. Tia Beatriz hurries forward to wrap the shawl more modestly around my shoulders. Lord Sales introduces us.

"King Henry, may I present Doña Juana of Spain, soon to be Archduchess of Burgundy. Doña Juana, this is my Lord Henry Tudor, King of England."

I sweep into a flowing curtsey, my eyes fastened to those of the English King. Then I giggle at the obvious awkwardness of my position, my hair wild and loose, clad only in my undershift and a borrowed shawl.

King Henry smiles gallantly in return as he bows. "When I heard that the ship of the Spanish princess was driven ashore,

I rode here as fast as I could. I thought Catherine, Princess of Wales, had arrived."

Lord Sales shakes his head. "No, my Lord, Lady Juana is the Spanish bride going to Burgundy. The storm scattered her wedding armada." He then proudly introduces the king to Doña Beatriz, who sweeps him a graceful curtsey.

The landlord and his wife are beside themselves with the honour of their royal visitor. They push the gawping crowd of villagers out of the door, to go back to their own homes, along with those of our Spanish retainers who will be lodged with them.

Yet more logs are added to the fire and Henry takes off his rain-soaked cloak and doublet, down to his shirt. Blankets are brought to wrap around Tia Beatriz and Lord Sales. A trestle table is set up before the fire and we eat venison, killed by King Henry and his hunting party, while the storm rages outside. I sit next to Henry, on his right side, and in a mixture of English and Latin, we talk easily and companionably.

Henry Tudor tells me of his queen, Elizabeth of York, and their four children, two boys and two girls. "All our children are well, by the grace of God."

I raise my rough clay beaker of ale in a salute to their health.

He searches my face. "Does your sister Catherine look like you?"

I smile. "No, my Lord. Catalina has blonde hair and blue eyes, like my mother. My brother Juan and I are the dark ones of our family."

He encourages me to tell him stories of my life growing up during the Granada War, and my home in the Alhambra.

He listens intently, fascinated. Then he tells me about himself, how he grew up in lonely exile in France, and his battles to win the throne of England. "Enough of war talk," he says. "Do you hunt?"

I nod, *yes*.

He switches to telling amusing tales about his hunting adventures. We find ourselves laughing out loud together, and the innkeeper replenishes the ale.

Lord Sales, seated on the king's left, is astonished to see the taciturn Henry Tudor joking and smiling like a young man in love.

The next day Henry and his entourage ride on to Winchester. I bid him farewell, and give him a tiny golden rosebud so skillfully worked that it looks real. He tucks it into his doublet. "Archduke Phillipe is a fortunate man," he says. "He has – in you – a treasure greater than gold."

✠

Two days later, our ship is repaired and we prepare to sail. Tia Beatriz bustles around, helping me. I am relieved to discover that my library of books, packed on board the ship, are safe. She smiles knowingly.

"Why did you worry that you would not be attractive to these men from the North, Juana? King Henry never took his eyes off you," she says. "Edmundo tells me that he can't remember seeing the king so talkative and relaxed and happy."

"Oh, Don Enrique" – I use the Spanish form of Henry – "is nice, but he is nearly as old as Papa." I think, *but his attention has already made me feel much more confident and desirable.* "I'm ready to meet Phillipe."

I learn from Tia Beatriz that Henry Tudor's marriage is a political one. Unlike my own father, Henry had taken no mistresses and sired no bastards.

"The Tudor hold on England is fragile; Henry can't afford to be fathering rival claimants to the crown," Lord Sales says.

Lord Sales and Tia Beatriz are pleased to see me smile, brightness returning to my cheeks and a revived sparkle in my eyes. *For the first time since leaving Spain, I feel like the girl that I had been at home.*

Doña Beatriz whispers to Lord Sales, "Having a man's – better yet a king's – undivided attention has worked wonders for Juana's spirits."

✠

With good sailing weather, it takes less than a day to cross the Channel from England to Flanders. We meet the other battered ships of the armada and learn that many of our caravels sank in the storm – including the one that carried my wedding dress. Tia Beatriz crosses herself when she hears the news, feeling as I do, that a bride's wedding gown at the bottom of the sea is a bad omen.

When we arrive at Antwerp, one of great city-states of Flanders, I see the townspeople and city dignitaries crowding the quay of the harbour, waiting to welcome me. I leave the ship with my entourage and we mount the big horses provided for us to parade into the city. I see the crowd divide, making way for Bishop Adrian Boyens. I shudder when I see him. He has grown fatter, wearing rich vestments and a great silver pectoral cross on a heavy chain. *But where is my bridegroom?* I pull my horse to a halt.

Lord Sales edges his horse closer to mine. "Archduke Phillipe will be here soon to meet you," he says confidently. He tries to divert my attention when he sees the pinched, anxious look on my face.

"We can always sail back to England," he says jokingly. "You've captured King Henry's heart."

When I remember the warm attention of the English king, I manage a smile.

"Here he is!" Lord Sales says as a fanfare of trumpets announce the arrival of the archduke, splendidly dressed and riding a white charger. I am enchanted by my first sight of him. What Phillipe Habsburg does next is so alien to protocol that it leaves Lord Sales open-mouthed in outrage.

Phillipe rides up to us, dismounts and boldly lifts me from my saddle. I am so surprised, that I offer him no resistance.

I think, *what a supremely confident, self-possessed young man he is!* As we stand facing each other, Phillipe takes off his glove and strokes my cheek. I almost forget to breathe.

"It pleases me that you are beautiful," he says in a low, melodious voice, looking directly into my eyes. He speaks in French, a language that I am still learning.

I stammer an inaudible reply; I don't know what has come over me. Phillipe's blonde good looks – his nickname of 'Phillipe the Fair is justly deserved – are a perfect counterfoil to my acknowledged dark beauty.

"Bishop Adrian?" Phillipe shouts, still eating me up with his eyes.

"Here, my Lord."

"Who is to marry us?"

"The cardinal, my Lord, at the formal wedding celebrations in Lille two days hence."

"Forget that, Bishop. I want you to marry us, immediately."

"But where? There is only the small fisherman's chapel…"

"That will do. Lead the way."

Lord Edmund Sales stands nearby, dumbfounded. It is obvious that in the few electric moments since I met Phillipe Habsburg, I have left Spain and my family, and England and King Henry Tudor far behind. I have forgotten about my wedding gown in its watery grave. I have forgotten about being young and shy and in a foreign land. It is like I was struck by a lightning-bolt; I see nothing but this handsome eighteen-year-old blonde-haired man, who wraps his arms around me and kisses me deeply in front of everyone.

To me, our hurried wedding vows are like a dream. The small chapel, the quick blessing and then Phillipe takes me by the hand and we run like children through the street to the bishop's house. There we spend our wedding night.

✠

In the early morning hours, awakened by the pealing of the bells, I stir from sleep and reach over to touch Phillipe. At the gentle brushing of my fingertips against his skin, he is instantly awake, making love to me again.

We spend the next two days in bed, in Bishop Adrian's own sumptuous palace; the bishop has vacated his residence to make room for us royal newlyweds. Phillipe orders the bishop's hovering servants away. He tells them not to disturb us, just leave meals outside the locked bedroom door for us, jugs of French wine and heavy Flemish beer.

In the early morning, pale sunlight from the open window touches Phillipe's hair, turning it to spun gold. I drink in the sight of his handsome profile, with the fine, blond bristles of his jawline catching the light. *I feel deliciously bewitched. I lose track of time and measure my life by his heartbeats.*

✠

Two days later, at our formal royal wedding at the Cathedral in Lille, Phillipe is barely able to keep his hands off me during the nuptial Mass. Because of the loss of my wedding dress, my bridesmaids and I wear our simple Spanish gowns that we still have with us.

After the cardinal's blessing, Phillipe and I depart to our new home, the ducal palace in Lille. Phillipe carries me down the corridor to the bedroom, my arms around his neck, both of us laughing with joy and anticipation. I remember seeing the faces of poor Lord Sales and Doña Beatriz in the cathedral during the wedding ceremony; Lord Sales standing grim and silent, and Doña Beatriz trying to smile through her tears.

That night I dream that Phillipe is with me in the gardens of the Alhambra, with the intoxicating, heavy scent of orange blossom and the ripple of the splashing fountains. I vow that I will take him to Granada one day.

"Granada? What's so special about Granada?" he drawls, when I wake him to tell him of my dream. "Oh, my sweet little Spanish savage, forget Granada. Flanders and Burgundy are so much better. I can't imagine living anywhere else; I'll never go to Granada. Burgundian style and fashion, this is the most sophisticated way to live; everything I want is right here, and I rule over it all."

He explains to me that his lands are diverse and scattered. In Flanders, he rules the prosperous wool-trading city-states of Antwerp, Bruges, Ghent and Lille, which he inherited from his mother. Further to the south, he claims as his mother's inheritance the sophisticated, stylish, French-speaking province of Burgundy, which Phillipe adores. He has grown up as ruling archduke from the age of five, when his mother was killed in the hunting accident. When I ask what he remembers of her, he shrugs.

His father? He says he has seen him two or three times in his life. Maximilian Habsburg lives in his own separate empire of Austria, and has little contact with his children in Flanders. When Maximilian dies, Phillipe will inherit Austria. I cannot image two families more different: we Trastamaras – parents and children – clinging together through war and peace, and the Habsburgs, who seem to be strangers related by blood.

Phillipe kisses my bare shoulder and plays with locks of my hair. "Don't worry about anything, my little Spanish mouse. Your only duty is look beautiful, and bear me sons."

Sons. At that word, I freeze. I remember the curse of Fatima, and her words: *"I wish this upon you: may your own son one day destroy you, as my son has destroyed me. One day you will have a son. And may he treat you as my son has treated me."*

"What the matter?" Phillipe asks, as he continues with a chain of kisses down my back.

"Nothing." His nearness drives away all other thoughts. He suddenly stops. "I don't want to hear your Spanish servants calling you Juana anymore. It's too foreign. Everyone must call you Joanna, it is much more suitable for the Archduchess of Burgundy."

"But Juana is what I was baptised."

"I like Joanna better. You will prefer it, in time. Just like you will prefer Burgundy."

I smile as I have seen my mother smile in arguments with my father. *Yes, everyone will call me Joanna. Yes, I will adapt to the ways of Burgundy. Then you must come with me to Granada, and I will make love to you in the gardens of the Alhambra.*

✠

"Hurry, it's time for the banquet." Bishop Adrian pounds on our bolted door. "All the great merchants of Flanders and the nobles of Burgundy are waiting to see their new archduchess in the Great Hall."

"We'll be with you shortly, Bishop," Phillipe calls back. He kisses me again.

"Let me get up," I protest. "I want to get dressed, to look my best for this."

"What will you wear? As my wife, you must appear as the most stunning woman at court."

"My best gown was lost in the storm at sea," I reply anxiously.

"Forget it; it was only a Spanish dress. I'm sure it wouldn't be fashionable enough." Phillipe orders his sister Margaret to give me one of her own gowns, cut in the Burgundian style. He also orders her to provide Burgundian gowns for my four

199

Spanish bridesmaids. Margaret, selfish and self-centered, is furious with her brother's demand. With bad grace, she tells her servant to dump the clothes at my door.

My bridesmaids and I are perplexed by the Burgundian-style gowns, for the skirts are in one section and the bodices separate.

"Which is the front and which is the back of this bodice?" I ask Tia Beatriz. "Surely it can't be worn this way around, my breasts will fall out. It must be this way, but the neck is extremely high."

"Better high and modest than cut so low. You would not even be decent with a lace shawl over it," my maid Teresa retorts, as she laces up the ribbons at the side.

Phillipe and his courtiers are already seated in the Great Hall when I enter with my bridesmaids in our borrowed finery; all eyes are on me. There is a moment of stunned silence, then the Flemish and Burgundian courtiers burst into shouts of laughter.

We modest Spanish girls have indeed put on the bodices back-to-front. Phillipe points at me, laughing so loud and hard he has difficulty catching his breath. At the high table, Margaret looks insufferably smug. Bishop Adrian joins in the merriment.

I blush crimson. *Why is Phillipe so obviously delighted to make me the butt of a joke in front of everyone? To make me feel so small and stupid?* I feel like crawling under the table and, at the far end of the hall, I see Lord Sales, face red with anger, there to witness my humiliation.

During the banquet, my eyes narrow as my young husband flirts boldly with the Flemish and Burgundian ladies of his court, who brazenly vie for his attention. I experience Burgundian style at its most ruthless ceremonial. I sit next to

Phillipe on the high dias, under a fringed canopy. Below us, on long tables, Bishop Adrian and the other members of the court are placed. Unlike meals in Spain, the serving and eating is a solemn and dreary affair.

The Burgundian musicians set up a kind of dirge in the background as each elaborate golden serving platter arrives, heaped with food constructed into fantastic forms of birds and animals; each is so intricately designed that you cannot guess what the original meat was.

The server first bows before us at the head table and the taster cuts off a slice of meat, ladling cupfuls of thick sauce over it. After he approves it, it is handed to Phillipe and to me. It is all congealed and cold by the time it reaches the table from the kitchen. There is no garlic, but a vast quantity of spices, all tossed in together, sweet and savory, and lots of pepper.

Spices and pepper are hugely expensive luxuries; I wonder how Phillipe's court can display so much wealth. *The Flanders wool trade is profitable, but surely it cannot bring in that much money. This ostentation could bankrupt a country.*

I watch Phillipe and carefully imitate everything he does with his eating and drinking vessels. I want to make sure I will do nothing to make him laugh at me in public again.

✠

By late February, 1497, the captains of the Spanish fleet have spent nearly five months in Antwerp harbour, and are anxious to return to Spain with Prince Juan's promised bride. Margaret Habsburg has started to use her Spanish title, insisting on being addressed as Margaret, Princess of the Asturias – but she shows no inclination of readying herself for the voyage.

The Spanish ships wait in vain with dwindling supplies, as the residents of Flanders feast and party throughout the Christmas season and into early spring. Phillipe takes me on a royal progress to each of his major cities: Lille, Bruges, Ghent.

I have ignored the letters from my parents and Juan, asking when Margaret is coming. I am able to think of nothing but Phillipe and his desires. He is like opium to me. But I am keen to see Margaret sail, for I like her even less than before, and I do not trust her after the incident with the borrowed dresses. I keep asking Phillipe to order his sister to board her ship, so the Spanish fleet can return home.

"Oh, Joanna," he says, never using my name Juana again. "Let Margaret stay a little longer, she adores parties."

After a visit to England with Doña Beatriz, Lord Sales returns to court in Flanders. He comes to me, angry, with the warning that the neglected and hungry crews of the Spanish ships are falling ill. It troubles me greatly, and I try to bring it to Phillipe's attention.

My husband's response is to shout at me, "Don't nag me about it, Joanna. We'll discuss things later, when I feel like it."

Lord Sales finally puts his foot down. Thousands of Spanish sailors and soldiers have died from the cold and Northern sicknesses, more are succumbing each day.

"We need to return to Spain, now." Lord Sales demands.

✠

Bishop Adrian stands near the fireplace in Margaret Habsburg's palace chamber. "My dear Princess of the Asturias, perhaps the time has come for you to go to Spain."

She sits on a cushioned chair in front of the fire and stares at him. "I don't want to go. From what I've seen of Joanna and her Spaniards, I'm going to hate it there. Did you know that Joanna prepared a private Christmas supper for me and Phillipe? She served us a revolting Spanish dish called *paella*, a ghastly mix of rice and olive oil, reeking of garlic. I gagged, and Phillipe refused to eat more than a spoonful."

"I'm sure your Prince Juan will be more accommodating. He's the most considerate young man."

"I've heard he and his sister are so alike, that King Fernando calls them 'the twins'.

"That was when they were children. They're adults now, and quite different." Bishop Adrian toys with large silver cross on his chest. "And besides, you will adore the jewels that Queen Isabel has ready for the bride of her beloved son and heir. The finest treasures of the Alhambra."

Margaret's eyes glow.

"I have something for you, too," Bishop Adrian says, withdrawing a small, rock-crystal bottle from the folds of his gown.

Margaret leans forward in her chair.

"When you get to Spain, it is vital that you have an heir immediately. Son or daughter, it doesn't matter. The Spanish succession can pass through either."

Margaret nods, the tip of her tongue darting between her lips.

Bishop Adrian shakes the bottle gently and hands it to her.

"Beginning on your wedding night, put a few drops of this into your bridegroom's wine. Continue each night until the bottle is finished."

"Just give it to him?" she asks. "None for me?" She holds the crystal to the firelight, the heavy fluid inside glowing like liquid opals.

"Once or twice won't kill you." He shrugs. "But don't make a habit of it."

She looks at her trusted guardian, Bishop Adrian, and nods. He has taught her well in the years since her mother's death. She slips the crystal vial into bodice, between her plump white breasts.

The Spanish fleet sets sail for home the first week in March, 1497, bearing Princess Margaret to the waiting Trastamara family.

✠

On board the Spanish flagship, Lord Edmund Sales and Doña Beatriz stand together at the rail, watching the sea as they leave the English Channel, sailing south.

"I worry about her, Edmundo," Beatriz says, slipping her arm into his.

"Who? That little minx Princess Margaret down in her cabin?"

"No, not her. It's Juana. My poor Juana. Phillipe made her send all of us away – her Spanish bridesmaids, her Spanish courtiers, her Spanish cook, her Spanish musicians, her Spanish servants. All Juana has left are the two girls, Teresa and Ana."

Edmund Sales nods savagely. *That damned Phillipe said he didn't want to see Doña Beatriz because he didn't like her scarred face.* Edmund gazes tenderly at Beatriz. She wears an black silk eyepatch and a Moorish-style headscarf, to conceal the side of her face torn by the *jihadi's* blade. He draws her closer to him, protectively.

"I wonder if sending her Spanish friends away was Phillipe's idea, or Bishop Adrian's? No matter, one's as bad as the other," Edmund says.

They stand together in silence, watching the seabirds wheeling overhead, before flying – one by one – back to land. "I worry for the whole Trastamara family. Phillipe Habsburg reminds me of something I saw as a boy, in England. Beatriz, have you ever seen a bird called a cuckoo?"

She looks puzzled.

"Let me tell you about the cuckoo. I was just a child when I saw this. I discovered a pair of wrens nesting in a tree next to my room. The two busy little parent wrens spent weeks building their nest of twigs, carefully lining it with their own feathers.

Then there were four tiny, perfect wren eggs in the cosy nest. Two days later, a cuckoo swooped in and laid its own large, speckled egg in the wren's nest. The wrens didn't seem to notice and the little mother wren sat on all the eggs and hatched them. As soon as it hatched, the cuckoo chick began pushing the baby wrens out of the nest, one by one, yet the two parent wrens kept bringing food to the monster that had destroyed their own children. They wore themselves out feeding it. The cuckoo chick had the biggest appetite, mouth always open, demanding more, more, more. I fear that the

Trastamara family – and Spain – are like the wrens, and Phillipe Habsburg is the cuckoo in their nest."

Beatriz shivers and is silent a long time. Then she squeezes his arm. "I can't bear to think about it. Come, the sun has gone. Let's go below."

✠

In each of the main cities of Flanders, Phillipe maintains an archducal palace. Two weeks after Margaret's departure, we are in the city of Bruge, where a chill night wind whistles down the canals of the city. The Flemish call Bruges 'the Venice of the North,' but I cannot imagine Venice being this cold.

I am alone in our palace bedroom, wrapped in my winter furs and huddled next to the fire. Freezing rain hammers at the window. *Where is Phillipe?* I shiver. *He is the only thing that keeps me warm.* It seems like forever since the ships sailed back to Spain; I miss hearing the familiar loud Spanish voices in the corridors, the Spanish songs and music, the food and jokes I shared with Tia Beatriz and my bridesmaids and my Castilian servants and courtiers.

I pace the room, waiting, waiting, waiting. *Where is Phillipe?* I feel a blind panic rise up like a wall in front of me. I try reading my prayer book, but the words refuse to focus. I hold the book between my palms, remembering the day Juan gave me this book before I sailed from Spain. *I know my brother remembers me in his prayers; but what will our respective marriages to these Habsburgs bring us?*

It is after midnight by the church bells when Phillipe

comes into the chamber, his breath heavy with wine.

"Where have you been?" I demand, frantic.

He stands swaying, looking at me with hooded eyes. "What, my little Spanish savage, are you my jailor now? And not even six months since our wedding?"

I fly at him, pounding my fists against his chest. I can smell the scent of another woman on his hands, his clothes. I tear the sleeve off his shirt and rip it to pieces. I throw the scraps to the floor and stamp them under my slippers.

Phillipe pushes me away from him and walks to the window. "My God, this room is hot. Why don't you get some fresh air?" He throws back the wooden shutters and the cold sleet whips into the room. I run to slam the shutters closed again, but he catches my wrists, stopping me. He pins me to him with one arm and uses his other hand to caress me, forcing a deep kiss on my mouth.

I struggle briefly, like an animal caught in a trap; an animal that first fights against the steel, then stops, resigned and accepting. I feel my body responding to him, melting against him, the desire to be part of him burning me like a shooting star in the night sky.

"Joanna, Joanna, my sweet…," he murmurs in my ear as he picks me up and carries me to the bed.

Then nothing exists but his kisses and his passion which again and again takes me beyond reason.

The wind and sleet howl through the open window, but I do not feel the cold any longer.

✠

Spring comes at last and in May I avidly read letters from home about the Spanish royal wedding of Juan and Margaret. It was held in April, 1497, in Burgos, the great Castilian city in northern Spain, in the splendid cathedral there. All Spain rejoices with our family.

My brother writes to tell me how happy Margaret makes him. Married life is bliss, he says. He plans to go to Seville soon, and take Margaret with him; he hopes that by the end of the year, she will be she with child, and that child will be born, as he was, in Seville.

His only concern, he writes, is the tightening grasp of the Inquisition; already, he has had one stormy confrontation with the Grand Inquisitor. Juan says that he will use his power as Prince of the Asturias, and royal heir, to curtail the Inquisition when he returns to Seville.

Juan and Margaret are now on their way to a second royal wedding, that of eldest sister Isabella. She is finally going to marry her persistent suitor King Manuel of Portugal. Juan adds at the end of his letter that Mama is exhausted from all the planning and preparation of two weddings in a row.

I miss Spain more than ever when I think of the weddings – Juan and Margaret, and Isabella and Manuel. I long to be there for the traditional *fiestas*: Spanish music, dancing, feasting, *corridas*.

My husband Phillipe shows no interest in the letters or the news from Spain. He repeatedly asks me why I am not yet pregnant. "What's wrong with you? Where is the son it is your duty to produce for me?"

✠

In Flanders, we move further inland, to the great merchant city of Lille, center of the wool trade. I try to adapt, but feel only contrasts to the home I left behind. Lille is noisy, with the constant rattle over the cobblestones of carts carrying wool from England; King Henry Tudor's merchants sends bales of raw wool across the Channel to Lille to be made into cloth. I run my hand over a bolt of the finished cloth – the fabric feels stiff and heavy, unlike the smooth, flowing Andalucian silks produced in Granada. The animals used for riding and to pull wagons are completely different than Spain. They don't have mules, so they harness big, heavily-muscled horses to pull the carts. In the city, the oily smell of wool pervades the air and the sound of clacking looms echoes down each street.

The townhouses of Lille are built with protruding jetties on their roofs, used to hoist bales of wool and the finished cloth into the upper stories for storage. The city people seem busy and determined when they work. When they drink, they drink to get drunk, becoming loud and boisterous. The most-admired women are the fat ones, with large white breasts and low-cut bodices to expose them. Adultery seems to them an amusing past time.

At the court of Flanders, the style of Burgundy is the fashion. There are no *corridas*, but tournament jousts on horseback for the nobility, and games played with leather balls for the peasants. *This is Phillipe Habsburg's world. Phillipe has several ornate suits of armor for the tournaments, but he has never fought in battle, has never been to war.*

I sit decoratively in the ducal pavilion to watch another

tournament with the ladies of the court. It is all bugles and flags and pageantry with mounted teams of noblemen; the shadow, not the substance, of battle. The life-and-death struggles of the Granada War, which formed my early existence, mean nothing to the people of Flanders. *I find that the Duchy of Burgundy is a world of pretense, a world that revolves around fun and fashion – should blue or yellow be worn this season? What feathers should trim this hat? Should sleeves this summer be tight or loose? I feel it could never be my world, as hard as I try to please my husband.*

✠

In the autumn, late October, 1497, I am enduring another banquet in the ducal palace in Lille. Between courses, I watch with distaste while my husband openly flirts with the ladies of the court.

I hear a disturbance at the back of the hall; a muddied courier pushes his way to the front, to the dais where Phillipe and I sit. I look up from my plate in astonishment, for the chief steward rarely allows anything to break the rigid protocol of a Burgundy-style feast.

From his cloak and his riding clothes, I see that the courier is Spanish. He shakes off the restraining arm of the Burgundian steward and draws his sword against the Flemish guards who rush forward to remove him from the hall.

"I have an important message for Doña Juana, news from Spain. I request a private audience immediately." He speaks in French, with a Spanish accent.

"Private?" my husband drawls. "Why private? I see no reason to keep secrets. Tell my whole court."

The courier bows and I see the muscles of his jaw tightening. "Please, my Lord, I was instructed to speak to Doña Juana alone."

"I said damn well tell my whole court!" Phillipe shouts and stands up. I sit back in my chair, and feel cold.

The messenger makes the sign of the cross. "I come at the behest of Queen Isabel of Castile and King Fernando of Aragon. They regret, with deepest sorrow, to tell Doña Juana that her brother, Don Juan, Prince of the Asturias, – the heir to the Kingdoms of Castile, Aragon, and Granada – is dead."

The hall goes silent and every eye is on me. I grip the armrests of my chair so tightly that it seems the bones of my hands will break. *I love my brother; he is my soulmate, my twin. All the years when we were growing up, with my father away at the war, and my mother too busy, Juan was my lifeline. Even now, in faraway Flanders, not a sun sets that I do not think of him. The bond between us can never be severed. And what of the Granada Prophecy? It has been foretold that without Juan, chaos will swallow Spain and the entire world. No, the words I have just heard cannot be true. Juan cannot be dead. Not my beloved twin, the pride and hope of Spain.*

The courier stands rigid, head bowed. My husband Phillipe sits back down in his chair and reaches for his goblet of wine. He drains it in a single gulp and looks over at me.

I stare straight ahead, unseeing.

Death. *Muerte.* The Spanish word sinks slowly into my heart, the way an anchor that is cut from its chain drops into the bottomless ocean. *My old nightmare of the ship in the storm, I see my brother release his grip on the rail and he slips beneath the waves.*

I rise slowly. I stand rigid, for an instant, then I violently sweep the table in front of me clear of all the dishes and goblets and carafes, sending them clattering and smashing to the floor. I put both my hands to the sides of my head, tearing off my jewelled headdress. I scream, a primeval howl of anguish torn from my soul, the otherworldly wail of a woman whose loved one is taken from her by death.

From the side of the hall, my maids, Teresa and Ana, rush to my side. Phillipe gestures for them to take me back to my chamber. The Spanish courier follows me.

Phillipe watches me depart, then he turns to his steward, orders more wine and summons Bishop Adrian Boyens to rise from his place at a lower table and join him. There is much to discuss. He signals to the musicians to begin again. The steward and servants sweep up the broken glass and debris. The Flemish and Burgundian guests in the hall begin an excited buzz of talk.

✠

I lay on my bed in the dark, numb and unseeing. Teresa holds my hand and sings softly in her own language, to comfort me. Ana stands by the door and I overhear her talking quietly to the Spanish courier.

"How did it happen?" she whispers.

"It is a mystery. Prince Juan was in perfect health at his wedding, and the honeymoon – well – it went on forever. The prince spent so much time in bed with his new wife that people began to joke about it. But then, on the 4th of October, he collapsed suddenly and died within hours. Queen Isabel did not even have time to reach him, but King Fernando was there."

Ana says, "Prince Juan was a truly good man. I fear what will happen to the New World in the future without him. How are the king and queen?"

"Devastated. The queen is especially stricken."

"As is Doña Juana. She told me that she and her brother are two halves of the same olive tree."

"I wanted to break the news to her more gently," the courier says sadly. "My orders are to wait here until Doña Juana is ready to send a reply back to her parents."

I hear Ana let him out through the door, which she closes and bolts when he is gone.

For the next week, I remain secluded, prostrate with grief. Phillipe is brusque. "If my wife is not well enough to see me, tell her I have better places to be."

✠

*My mind goes back to the 4th of October, when I had awakened with a nightmare, a terrible premonition. Phillipe was out again, as he often was, and I was sleeping alone. My cry brought Teresa and Ana running to me.*

"Can you hear it?" I demanded, struggling out of bed to the window, which I flung open. Moonlight poured into the room.

"No, my Lady, I hear nothing," Teresa said soothingly, trying to lead me back to bed.

"I can hear it – it's Juan's greyhound, Bruto," I cried. "Remember? The dog I gave him as a puppy, his favourite," I turned to Teresa, distraught. "Surely you can hear it? It's

Bruto. He's howling, you must hear it."

"No, my Lady, no. You are dreaming. Wake up, wake up now. You could not hear the dog crying this far away from Spain."

✠

My eyes are closed, my head heavy on the pillow. Into the aching emptiness of my mind comes the sound of church bells pealing loudly, over and over, for a long time. I stir on the bed and open my eyes. Ana appears at my side.

"The bells, Ana? The cathedral bells are ringing?"

"Yes, my Lady. The bells of Lille cathedral, and all the churches of the city."

I take a deep breath. I bite my lip and say with sad resignation, "It must be the memorial service for Juan..."

Ana looks anxiously from me to Teresa. "No, my Lady. The bells are to announce the coronation."

"The coronation?" I struggle to sit up.

"Bishop Adrian Boyens has decreed that with the death of Prince Juan, your husband Phillipe is to be crowned 'Prince of the Asturias', heir to the thrones of Castile and Granada. Church bells across Flanders are ringing for Phillipe's coronation service."

"Is he mad?" I scream. "Phillipe can never take Juan's place!"

Ana murmurs, "Bishop Adrian has decreed that, since the next heir to Castile is your sister Isabella and because she is already Queen of Portugal, the title of 'Prince of the Asturias' should go to Phillipe."

214

"No. No. Never!" I say with fire in my voice, rising from my bed and taking the robe Teresa holds out for me. "Is the Spanish courier that my parents sent still here?"

"Yes."

"Tell him to come immediately. I have a message for him to take to Spain."

King Fernando and Queen Isabel are furious when they hear the news of Phillipe and his attempts to usurp the title 'Prince of the Asturias'. In a blazing letter to Phillipe, Isabel declares:

The succession to my Kingdom of Castile, with its subsidiary Kingdom of Granada and my New World territories, is quite clear. After my beloved son Prince Juan, my eldest daughter Isabella is my heir. Isabella is now both Queen Consort of Portugal, and Princess of the Asturias. She is my heir to Castile, Granada, and the New World. Next in the line of succession will be any children Isabella may have. Third in the line of succession would be my daughter Doña Juana. You have absolutely no claim to the Castilian inheritance, Phillipe; you are merely Doña Juana's consort.

Bishop Adrian reads the letter aloud that Phillip angrily handed to him.

"I will go to Spain myself," the bishop says soothingly. "I will talk to the queen in person about the succession and make her see the wisdom of our decision."

"Please do so at once."

"And, my Lord, I will personally escort your sister back home to Flanders. Margaret has resumed her former title of Duchess of Burgundy. It is unfortunate, but she had a miscarriage five weeks after Prince Juan's funeral."

"I wonder if you can find her another rich husband?" Phillipe muses.

✠

I am not left alone in Flanders to mourn through the months of the dark cold winter of 1497. From Spain, Lord Edmund Sales comes to be with me. He stops in England first, to confer with King Henry Tudor. My dear Don Edmundo, little by little, begins coaxing me back to life. He is appalled by the way Phillipe treats me and reports this to King Henry.

King Henry takes an exceptional interest in my welfare. He is also in communication with Phillipe, trying to get his signature on a new commercial wool-trading treaty. Wool is a vital part of the English economy, for the English sell tons of raw fleeces to Flanders for processing into cloth.

By the spring of 1498 and the good sailing weather, Lord Sales makes ready to return to Spain. We are walking in the garden, speaking privately.

"King Henry says you are always to remember his great concern for your welfare. With your sister Catalina as Princess of Wales, he considers you as part of his family, too."

"I'm grateful. I miss my family."

"Juana, you must be careful. Remember, in the early days in Granada, I told you to trust no one. That is even more important here."

I start to interrupt him, but he puts a finger to his lips for silence. "Your maid Ana has told me how Phillipe treats you – the other women, how he locks you in your room and won't let you speak to visitors from Spain. And your money – that he has taken control of your allowance and turned it over to a Flemish controller, only doling you out a pittance to live on. Worst of all are the reports that he strikes you when he is angry. No, don't try to defend him. He is an arrogant young pup, spoiled since he was elevated to archduke as a child. He is tyrant to his servants, fawned over by his courtiers, and Father – sorry, now Bishop – Adrian Boyens pulling the strings behind the scenes. King Henry does not like him, or trust him. Henry has spies here in Phillipe's court and he says that the letters you write to Spain are intercepted by Phillipe and never get to your parents. Only Phillipe's side of the story, claiming that you have become unbalanced since your brother died."

"What about Ana and Teresa? Can I trust them?"

"You can trust Ana and Teresa with your life," he says firmly. "They are completely devoted to you. Ana is in contact with King Henry's courier."

"My husband Phillipe hates Ana and Teresa. He calls them my 'Moorish slave girls' and wants me to get rid of them."

"Phillipe won't move against Ana and Teresa, not without endangering his own life, quite frankly. He fears their native powers, and with good reason. Keep them close to you."

I nod in agreement.

"I must go to my ship now." He kisses me tenderly on both cheeks and hugs me. He seems close to tears as he takes something, wrapped in a soft leather pouch, from his doublet. He says firmly, "Let no one see this, it is for you alone."

217

I open the pouch, and the great ruby jewel of Granada tumbles into my hand; the ruby I had first seen in King Boabdil's turban, that he had entrusted to Juan, the promise to protect the legacy of the Alhambra.

"The last time I saw your brother, he said to give this to you. He said you would understand, without words."

I nod my head. *Yes, I understand*. "I will miss you, dear Don Edmundo. Please, when you get back to Spain, go to my brother's tomb. Light a candle for me. Juan was the light of my life."

"He was the light of all Spain," Lord Sales replies, his words breaking. "We face a dark future without him."

✠

After Lord Sales leaves, Phillipe promises me that he will change his selfish ways, stop his womanising, never strike me again and become an attentive and loving husband. I believe his promises and pray that our life will be different now.

From Spain comes the news that my sister Isabella is pregnant, with her baby expected in the summer. Then I discover that I, too, am pregnant. To the mourning Trastamara family, it seems that the promise of these new lives is a blessing after the great sadness of bereavement. Phillipe is jubilant, convinced that my baby will be a boy. Troubled by the memory of Fatima's curse, I pray daily that the child I am carrying will be a girl.

✠

The delivery is difficult and protracted, but my sister Isabella, Queen of Portugal and Princess of the Asturias, gives birth to a son on the 24th of August, 1498, at my father's palace in Zaragoza. An hour later she dies in Queen Isabel's arms.

Our Trastamara family is again plunged into grief and Queen Isabel feels that God no longer answers her prayers. There are those who say that had our Jewish family physician Doctor Badoc still been in Spain, he could have saved Isabella's life, and Juan's life, too.

Bishop Adrian Boyens waits outside the palace gate, like a vulture at a carrion pit. "Please give Queen Isabel and King Fernando my condolences on their daughter's death," he tells Archbishop Cisneros. "And give them my congratulations on the birth of their grandson, Miguel."

Bishop Adrian rides to Burgos to collect Margaret Habsburg. Together they will sail back to Flanders. As he begins his journey, Bishop Adrian considers his next move on the chessboard. *Now only one tiny, newborn baby boy stands between Joanna and Phillipe Habsburg and the Castilian inheritance. This inheritance encompasses the gold of Granada and the promise of New World riches; it will bring wealth and power beyond the dreams of any king that ever lived.*

✠

After an easy pregnancy and a quick labour, I give birth to my first child on November 15th, 1498. The celebrations in Bruge are cancelled. The baby's Habsburg grandfather, Emperor Maximilian, who was on the road to Flanders to attend the christening, returns to Austria when he hears the news. It's only a girl, not the son and heir.

The disappointment of the Flemish and Burgundian courtiers is palpable. *My beautiful, healthy baby is a girl. Only a son can inherit. A daughter is worthless to them, but not to me.*

Phillipe is not pleased. He scarcely glances at the infant when the Flemish midwife tells him he has a daughter. He stands by my bed and tells me that because it is a girl, I can keep the baby with me for one week. Then little Eleanor, as she has been named, is to be be sent away.

"Why?" I ask Phillipe. "Why will you take my baby away from me?" I hold her to my breast, bonding immediately with my precious little one. I am so pleased and relieved to have a daughter.

"How many times do I have to tell you, Joanna? It is the Burgundian custom that our babies are sent away to be raised in their own households. As a Habsburg, my daughter Eleanor will have her own separate court, her own courtiers and her own servants."

I remember royal family life in Spain; how my mother and father kept us children together with them, throughout the Granada War. No matter how far we traveled, we remained a united family – across the mountains and *mesetas* of Spain from Valladolid to Toledo, to Seville, to Cordoba, to Malaga and on to Granada.

I glare at him defiantly, holding my baby even tighter. "Eleanor stays with me, it is the custom of royal mothers in Spain. I will nurse all my babies for their first weeks of life, as my mother did. I will guide their first steps, teach them their first words."

"You are not in Spain."

He signals to one of the hovering Flemish servants, but I defy anyone to pry her from my arms. "If you take Eleanor way, I will refuse to eat."

My husband acknowledges the threat in my eyes. "Very well, Joanna. I will make an exception from Burgundian protocol, just this once. You can keep the baby with you for two weeks before she is sent to her own household. Then, after you give me a son, Eleanor can be raised by you as you wish. But first, you must give me a son and heir."

✠

I miss my baby dreadfully, and fall into a deep depression, which Phillipe pretends not to notice. The care and devotion of Ana and Teresa encourage me to survive; on a sunny day, in early autumn, 1499, I am sitting in the garden when Ana comes quietly to my side, and passes me a letter. She hands it to me surreptitiously, having hidden it in a basket of apples. It is from my sister Maria, and I carefully slip the letter between the pages of the book I had been reading. No one sees me. I devour the news from Spain:

Dearest Sister,

I am writing to you from the Alhambra Palace. We have not received any letters from you all spring and summer. Maybe your letters have been lost at sea? I hope you are well.

Mama, Catalina and I have returned to Granada, where Mama has decided to raise Isabella's baby. He is named Miguel de la Paz,

221

'Michael of Peace', because he is the bond between Spain and Portugal. He has the Spanish title of 'Prince of the Asturias', and he is also 'Crown Prince of Portugal'. He is such a dear little baby, he doesn't realise how important he is! I think it is sad that he will never know his mother, who died when he was born. Mama and Papa were heartbroken over Isabella's death. And her poor husband, King Manuel of Portugal.

Her husband loved Isabella very much. He is such a kind man; he agreed to leave the baby with Mama in Granada and he went back to Lisbon all alone. He begs me for news of his little boy, and he writes me all the time and sends gifts. He has asked me to take special care of his son for him. He will arrive next week for little Miguel's first birthday. When Miguel is older, he will go to Portugal to live with his father, the king, in Lisbon.

Papa is not with in Granada, he has gone to Italy. There is more trouble with his dominions there.

Oh, Juana, you should see Miguel de la Paz! I call him by the affectionate diminutive, *Miguelito*, little Miguel. He is the most wonderful baby, he is so gentle and has the happiest smile. He notices everything around him. He is small for his age, but Mama says that I was small too when I was a baby, and look what a big girl I have become! I will be sixteen this year.

I wish you and your baby Eleanor were here,

so I could hug and kiss her. We were so happy when we got the news that she was born. She must be beautiful, just like you. How lovely having a daughter of your very own. I envy you. I think of you cuddling her and nursing her and playing with her and having her with you all the time. I can hardly wait to marry and have babies of my own! Is it true? We have heard a happy rumour that you are pregnant again!

My writing is not as good as yours and I am sorry for all the blotches of ink on the paper. I am writing at a table that has been set up in the Courtyard of the Lions; Miguelito is sleeping in his cradle near me.

It is a pleasant afternoon and Mama says the fresh air is good for the baby. I can look over and see his dear, tiny, little face. I love cuddling him and holding him in my arms as I take him for walks around the gardens of the Alhambra. Wouldn't it be wonderful if you and your little Eleanor could be here with us? We would have such a good time playing with the babies. We could take them up to the Generalife gardens where it is cooler, and let them splash in the fountains.

Mama adores Miguelito, of course. She spends as much time with him as she can. I thought she would never smile again after our brother Juan died, but when baby Miguelito was still tiny, he grabbed her outstretched finger and gurgled happily at her; Juana, I saw Mama smile.

It is good having Don Edmundo Sales here and Doña Beatriz. She came to be with Mama after Isabella died. We were so worried about you being alone in Flanders after Juan died; Don Edmundo volunteered to go to support you.

He wants to marry Doña Beatriz, but they cannot. They will have to wait seven years, since the time her husband, Don Sebastian de Leyva, was missing-in-action during the war. Then the church will declare her free to marry again.

I cannot believe our brother Juan is gone. You and Juan were always 'the twins' to me. Now I have only one of you left, so far away in another country. I keep thinking I see you and Juan in the gardens here, and when I wake up from my siesta, that I will see Juan coming into the room I shared with you, laughing the way he used to laugh, like golden bells tinkling. In the evening, at sunset, I listen to the fountains playing and I think I can hear the music of Juan's guitar. Then I rush to Miguelito's crib (he sleeps in the same room as Mama) and pick him up and hug him, smelling his special, warm baby smell, and I feel better.

I see that Miguelito has woken up. He is looking at me and smiling. He wants me to pick him up and hold him, so I end the letter now.

Please write. Mama worries about you, and I do also. The Spanish ambassador in Lille sends Mama letters through the Spanish ambassador in London

224

when they hear anything about you. Please write soon.

Give your darling little Eleanor a big hug and kiss from her loving Auntie María.

*Besos,*

Your sister, María de Trastamara

✠

It is snowing outside my window in Ghent: February 24th, 1500. I lean back into the pillows as my maid Teresa lifts a drink to my lips. My husband Phillipe and Bishop Adrian stand at the foot of my bed, watching the Flemish midwife as she sponges my baby down, then wraps the squirming little body in cloth-of-gold. I hear the newborn mewing in protest at the feel of the scratchy fabric.

The midwife passes the infant, not into my outstretched arms, but into the stiff hands of the bishop. Holding the baby, he turns and bows formally to Philippe.

"My Lord, a son. Your heir."

Phillipe beams. He takes the baby and cradles him against his chest, pulling down the cloth-of-gold wrapping to assure himself that it is indeed a boy.

"Phillipe, give me my baby. Please." I again hold out my arms.

Philip smiles at me, the smile that I feared I would never see again in his eyes when he looked at me.

"Well done, Joanna." He turns to leave the chamber, still holding the infant.

I struggle to rise from the bed. The midwife and her

225

Flemish assistants push me back down. I am strong, for this birth, like that of Eleanor, was easy. I was only in labour for six hours; prior to that, I was at a dance and, caught up in the magic of the music, I danced in spite of the disapproving glances and pursed lips of the Flemish and Burundian courtiers.

I did not suffer at all during my pregnancy, my condition not even showing on my slender frame until the fifth month.

Bishop Adrian says, "This boy is the heir of Burgundy and Flanders and also the heir of his grandfather the Holy Roman Emperor. He is too important to be left with you."

"Left with me?" I push my tumbled dark hair back from my face. "I am his mother!" I sit upright, careful not to antagonise the Flemish midwife and her helpers.

"And I am his father." Phillipe pauses in the doorway and turns to face me. "He is a Habsburg, and the heir of the Habsburgs."

I try to keep my voice steady. "You promised me, you promised that this baby could stay with me and I could have Eleanor back, too."

Phillipe shakes his head. "The doctor thought we should humour you during the pregnancy. But now that my son is safely delivered, he will go immediately to his own palace in Lille, with his wet nurse and his lord chamberlain to oversee his staff. He will be christened Charles, after my mother's father."

"But I thought we agreed on the name Juan – I mean John – after my brother?" My husband frowns when I use the Spanish name.

"Did I agree to that? I don't remember it. By the way, my sister Margaret will be his godmother."

Teresa hovers near my side, stoking my hair and trying to soothe me.

"What about Eleanor?" I plead. "What about my little girl? Can she live with me now?"

"I will think about it," he replies coldly.

For the past eighteen months, I have only been able to see my precious little daughter on rare public occasions. The tiny child, dressed in resplendent robes, was brought before the court and paraded around the assembly like a stuffed peacock on a gold plate – one of the ceremonial dishes of a formal Burgundian banquet. Her purpose was to show that I was capable of childbearing, of producing the required son and heir.

*Burgundy.* I spit out the word in my mind. *Everything done the Burgundian way. A world built on a façade of ceremony, nothing real.*

"I want to go home."

"You are home," Phillipe says.

"I want to go back to Spain, with my babies."

I hear his laughter as he walks out the door.

"Phillipe, wait," I beg from the bed. "We could go to Spain together." He acts as if he doesn't hear me. Bishop Adrian waves a hand toward the Flemish attendants and turns to follow Philippe, who carries our son, swaddled in cloth-of-gold. He signals the guard to close the door. In honour of the birth of the heir, Adrian Boyens is to be elevated to the title of archbishop.

I lay back in my bed, weeping softly. *My son. The son whose birth I have feared since a moonlit night at the Alhambra, at the curse of an old woman, is born. But in the nine months of carrying him and during his easy birth, I felt only an overpowering love for this baby. Surely the curse of Fatima is powerless against the force of my love?*

Teresa brings me another drink, herbs of her own preparation, and I fall asleep.

I dream again of the Alhambra. I see myself in the Generalife gardens, seated on a comfortable *almohada*, cradling my newborn son against my breast. My sister Maria arrives, bringing Miguelito and my own little Eleanor to join us. Maria sits down next to me. We watch the two little cousins, Miguelito and Eleanor, toddling happily hand-in-hand around the courtyard, and we laugh as they harmlessly chase the white doves that come to drink in the fountain. Teresa and Ana, and our Spanish servants gather to admire the children, *"Que quapa, que quapo,* how beautiful," they say encouragingly, clapping their hands. In my dreams, I live again with the sounds and scents and sunshine of a world that I fear I have been exiled from forever.

✠

Dearest Sister,

We received the letter from Phillipe in the spring, announcing the birth of your baby Charles, that is *Carlos*, in Spanish. We have never had a 'Carlos' in the family before, but any name is a good name for a blessed baby. It is good to hear that he is a big healthy boy.

The weather is getting hot again this summer — it is July now — but it is cool in the Alhambra Palace. Don't say anything to Mama, but I am worried about Miguelito. He has started walking, but he gets tired easily. He still tries to be cheerful, even when cutting his teeth. He is eating soft fruits now and the nurses are still feeding him, but he isn't putting on much weight.

Last month, Archbishop Adrian Boyens arrived in Granada for a visit. He is a very knowledgeable man, and he says not to worry about Miguelito, he will think of something to help him.

Did you get Papa's letter? He wants you to come back to Spain and bring both Eleanor and Carlos with you. It will be so good to have you home with us again, and Mama wants so much to have all her grandchildren here with her. I want you to come home, too.

Besos,
    Your sister, Maria

✠

The archbishop's ship catches the fastest winds from Spain back to Flanders. When he lands in Antwerp in September, 1500, Adrian Boyens rides quickly to Bruges and immediately goes to Phillipe's chamber.

"The baby Prince of the Asturias is dead," Archbishop Adrian announces. "Queen Isabel asked me to help him, but alas, there was nothing I could do. They buried him in the royal chapel of the Alhambra. Such a tiny coffin."

Phillipe signals to a servant to pour wine for them.

"I left Spain after the funeral," Archbishop Adrian continues. "It seemed as if the heart of Spain had stopped beating. Portugal too went into mourning for their little lost Trastamara prince. Queen Isabel is bereft. King Fernando rushed back from Italy to be at her side."

"And now?" Phillipe asks, taking a deep drink of his wine.

"Queen Isabel has proclaimed Joanna as 'Princess of the Asturias'. Your wife is the heiress to the Kingdom of Castile, Granada, and the New World. Isabel and Fernando agreed to sign a document acknowledging you as prince."

"Do you mean I'll be Joanna's 'Prince Consort', or do they accept me as ruling Prince of the Asturias?"

"For now, Prince Consort. Time is on your side, after all, you are only twenty-three years old. Isabel and Fernando say that if you come to Spain with Joanna and the children, they will discuss your role further."

Phillipe snorts derisively. "They're still trying to command the world, I see. Well, things have changed; I've got Joanna in Flanders, and their only grandchildren, Charles and Eleanor, in Flanders, and I'm in no rush to go to Spain. Isabel and Fernando can wait until I'm ready."

"When do you think that might be, my Lord?"

"Maybe next year. I have important business pending here. While you were in Spain, I opened negotiations for a new treaty with the English wool merchants and King Henry Tudor has invited me to a meeting with him."

✠

In Bruge, I receive the news of my baby nephew Miguel's death with a steely resignation. I ask Ana and Teresa to leave me, and I stand at the window of my chamber; the moon is full, turning the canal below my casement to silver. I look up to the stars in heaven. Does King Henry Tudor watch the same moon in England? Does he think of me? Does the same moon shine into the courtyards of the Alhambra tonight? What do my grieving parents pray for now, as they place their candles at the tomb of little Miguel de la Paz? I touch the cover of my prayer book, Juan's last gift to me.

I remember again, the eagle of my patron, San Juan. The eagle, the only creature able to stare into the face of the sun. I have stared into the sun. And I still live.

I am Juana, Princess of the Asturias. Heiress of the Kingdom of Castile, and Heiress of the New World across the Atlantic.

I am Heiress of the golden Kingdom of Granada. *My brother Juan's crown has come to me, and I swear to him with every fibre of my being: "I will fight to fulfill your dreams for Spain. I promise to rule Spain as you would have ruled, my dearest twin. I will try, with the help of God, to stave off the darkness left in a world without you."*

The scent of rosemary, the remembered fragrance of that long-ago day with my brother in the gardens of the Alhambra, fills the room.

✠

I am pleased when, in December, 1500, King Henry Tudor invites Phillipe to travel to England, to seal their new trade agreement between the English wool suppliers and the cloth manufacturing states of Flanders. King Henry plans a great celebration with a tournament – always dear to my husband's heart.

When he receives the formal invitation from King Henry, Phillipe accepts with alacrity, then tells the waiting English courier, "My wife Joanna will stay in Flanders. She's still mourning the death of her little nephew, Prince Miguel."

"King Henry will be very disappointed if the Princess of the Asturias does not come. His queen will be at the ceremonies, after all."

Phillipe sighs and agrees with great reluctance that I be included.

After the courier leaves, I challenge Phillipe. "Are you afraid I'll escape you once I'm in English territory?" I gently touch two fingertips to my cheekbone, where a bruise rises where he slapped me during another argument over his latest mistress. I long for the protection of my dear friend Lord Edmund Sales.

"You won't try anything." Phillipe retorts. "You'll travel quietly to England and back home with me, as my loyal wife. Remember that Archbishop Adrian will be keeping the children in Lille."

It begins to snow when Phillipe and I board our ship at Antwerp, bound for the English port of Dover, just across the Channel. The sailing, with good winds, takes less than eight hours. Then up the Thames and we travel on horseback to Windsor Castle.

My husband and I ride, side by side and in silence, at the head of our entourage. The snow continues to fall, but I am wrapped in furs and warm on my beautifully caparisoned horse. There is a new addition to my personal entourage, for my father has sent a group of Spanish musicians – who served in my brother Juan's court – to play the music of my homeland, to lift my spirits. I insisted that my Spanish musicians pack their instruments and travel with me to England.

The walls of Windsor Castle, seen from the distance, remind me of the Alhambra on its hill, the falcon's nest of stone. The snowdrifts lie in soft rolls, like new wool, over the battlements. The trees are like brushstrokes of black calligraphy on white parchment.

*I remember the day the snow fell, on the day my family rode into Granada, and how I watched the snowflakes melting on my new gloves.* I smile wistfully at the memory and raise my glove from the reins to my cheek. The bruise is diminishing and Teresa has attempted to conceal it with rice powder.

From Windsor Castle, King Henry Tudor and his entourage ride out to greet us. I have not seen him since the time my ship was blown ashore in England, en route to my wedding in Flanders. I was a girl then; now I am a woman of twenty-one, and a mother.

"Welcome, Prince Phillipe and Princess Juana."

I hear Phillipe swear under his breath when he hears Henry use my Spanish name, *Juana*, instead of Joanna. I lower my eyes, then raise them to look at Henry, who sweeps off his hat in a courtly gesture. It looks like a new hat, adorned with a white ostrich feather curling over its brim; a suitor's hat.

Henry's face is thinner then when I last saw him, more chiseled, the lines worn deeper across his forehead and down toward his mouth. His hair is threaded with grey. He sits easily in the saddle, wiry and fit as a man half his age.

"It is good to see you again, my Lord." I say in English. There is a brightness in my voice that has not been heard for a long time.

"Have you received the splendid news from Spain, from our friend Lord Edmund Sales?" he asks. "He and Doña Beatriz are married!"

I smile in relief and happiness. "At long last she is free to marry the man she loves. Please, my Lord, when you write to Lord Sales and Doña Beatriz, send them my best wishes and my love."

"I will." Henry replaces his hat, still looking at me. I see him wince when he notices the bruise on my cheek, but who can confront a husband for what he does to his wife?

We ride back through the castle gates together. As is the custom in northern courts, I have my separate chambers from my husband. Phillipe tells Henry that I will stay in my room, claiming it is the custom of Spanish mourning.

There are two days of treaty negotiations, followed by two days of a jousting tournament. Phillipe is in his element; he is the honoured guest. He and King Henry sign their treaty, and his Burgundian team win the jousting tournament.

The night before we leave to return to Flanders for Christmas, there is to be a great banquet. I am determined to attend. In my chamber, I sigh and smooth my hair in the mirror. "Tonight is King Henry's banquet. What have you brought me to wear?"

Ana and Teresa hover in attendance. "Here is your black velvet gown, suitable for mourning," Teresa says. I see her shoot a conspiratorial smile at Ana. "But we also packed your amethyst silk gown, cut in the Moorish style."

"And King Boadil's ruby, to wear as a brooch," Ana adds.

I study my reflection in the mirror. "Tonight, I set aside mourning," I say firmly. "I will celebrate the English king's hospitality, and I will dance for him as a tribute." Teresa brushes my hair so vigorously that blue sparks fly into the air. My eyes glow. "Yes. I'll say that my confessor has given me dispensation."

The banqueting hall of Windsor Castle is alight with a thousand candles when I enter. My husband stares, open-mouthed, when he sees me. The English head steward hurriedly arranges a chair and place setting for me, next to King Henry.

The banquet is fabulous. The English wool merchants and courtiers are astonished that Henry Tudor is spending this kind of money to entertain his guests. He has a reputation for being extremely frugal.

I am seated on King Henry's right side, and his wife, Queen Elizabeth, a pale cipher, sits listlessly next to Phillipe. When the time comes for dancing, the last crumbs of the feast are cleared, the trestle tables are dismantled and taken away and the English musicians appear. King Henry watches dutifully as his queen steps through a stately reel with the Duke of Norfolk.

I turn to King Henry. "My Lord, to thank you for your gracious hospitality, I shall dance for you."

"Joanna!" My husband's warning growl. "Remember you are in mourning."

I ignore him. "Can you play the music of Spain?" I ask the English musicians as I stand up. Surprised, they confer among themselves. "I'm not certain, my Lady," their leader says respectfully.

I clap my hands. "Then let my own musicians come to play for us! Join in with them, music master! Let us all hear the songs of Granada."

The Spanish musicians enter the hall and sit in a semi-circle. The guitars begin, the tambourines, the singer's voice rising, then the staccato *palmas*, the clapping hands of flamenco. Several of the English musicians find the rhythm and join in. The audience of English courtiers and merchants are mesmerised with delight.

The Spanish musicians finish this introduction with a flourish; the English courtiers in the banqueting hall and the servants, crowding into the doorways to listen, applaud wildly in appreciation.

Then the guitars began again in earnest, the rhythm seductive and demanding. I take off my jewelled headdress, hand it to Ana, and shake my long, dark hair loose over my amethyst gown. I step into the center of the semi-circle. The music, as always, engulfs my soul as it weaves its magic. I become a burning fire like the ruby as I dance, my hands and arms flowing into graceful curves of movement, my feet tapping the beat of the music.

I toss my head and, through a tress of hair that sweeps across one eye, I catch a glimpse of Henry watching me. In my dance, each sensuous step, each graceful beckoning gesture, awakes something that he has long struggled to suppress.

I see Henry Tudor as he was when he was a young man, during the years of his own exile from England; during the terrible war between rival English contenders for the crown and the compromises Henry forced himself to make to become King of England.

The candlelight shimmers over my skin and hair and the flowing curves of my amethyst silk gown. It catches the fire inside King Boabil's ruby. I half-close my eyes and I lose myself in the dance.

The music reaches a crescendo and I pause for a count of the beat. I instinctively feel every muscle of my body tense, like a bowstring drawn to its furthest reach before the arrow flies.

The music stops. I make a deep curtsey and return to my chair by Henry's side, my ears ringing with applause from the English guests. My husband Phillipe turns away from me, his mouth a slash of disapproval.

Henry leans toward me and I hear him take a deep breath, as he inhales my fragrance. He draws in to the farthest reaches of his mind this glorious, mysterious, oriental scent.

There is, like dew on the grass, a glow on my skin. Henry dares to reach over and touch the back of my hand as it rests on the tabletop. "You are the most beautiful woman in the world," he whispers in my ear. I hold my head straight as Ana gathers my hair into thick knot at the nape of my neck, replacing my headdress like a crown.

"Thank you, my Lord. They say my great-grandmother, Merina de Cordoba, was the most beautiful woman in the world; perhaps I take after her."

I glance down at his hand over mine, then look up and smile – a conspirator's smile – into his eyes.

☨

The next morning Phillipe announces that we will return at once to Flanders. King Henry and his courtiers accompany us to Dover, where we board our ship in the harbour. The weather still holds, crisp and clear, a perfect wind for a quick voyage across the English Channel.

My husband Phillipe gruffly says his goodbyes to our host and retreats to our cabin below. I remain on deck as the sails are hoisted, looking back to see Henry on the shore. He moves away from his courtiers and stands alone, watching me.

The ocean wind stings my eyes, and, as the ship surges away, I see his form growing smaller in distance that separates us. I feel an exhilarating sense of destiny. *The year 1500 is almost over, yet the world has not come to an end, as the doomsayers foretold in my childhood. But perhaps my world has.*

I raise my hand in farewell to the English king.

This is not goodbye, my dear, *querido*, but my promise. I will see you again.

# Historical Note

The *Granada Gold* cover looks like Juana Trastamara, based on the portrait of her that I saw in her own 15th Century Psalter – an illuminated manuscript – on display in the British Library, London.

Juana Trastamara went down in history as Queen *Juana La Loca* – a legend in Spain – and Joanna the Mad, according to her Habsburg husband. Enemies claimed that she lost her mind when her husband Phillipe died; her son, Charles, said his mother was mentally unfit, so he could take her throne for himself and lock her away.

Many historians today doubt the 'Mad Queen' label. So do I. A royal eyewitness of the time, King Henry Tudor of England, met Juana personally and declared that he found her completely sane – ("in spite of what her husband says", Henry writes.), He was obviously attracted to the beautiful Juana, and – after both their respective spouses were dead – he announced his intention to marry her.

The key people and incidents in the book are historically documented. I studied primary manuscripts and over forty reference books by other historians, plus exploring the cities and countryside in Spain where the action occurs.

My historical *facts* are like the genuine gemstones on a

necklace, and the historical *fiction* is the chain binding them together.

**Fact:** Lord Sales was an English nobleman who went to Spain to help the Christians in the Granada War. There was a troop of English archers who fought in Spain, too; somewhat like the English 'International Brigades' during the 1930's Spanish Civil War.

**Fact:** Adrian Boyens was the center of an international web of power and intrigue. He rose from a modest Flemish family to mastermind the Habsburg takeover of Spain; he would later become Grand Inquisitor of the Spanish Inquisition (during its most ruthless phase), Regent of Spain, and eventually, Pope Adrian.

**Fact:** Prince Juan Trastamara, the bright hope of a united Spain, died young on his honeymoon – poison was suspected.

**Fact:** The Prophecy, which I have dubbed 'The Granada Prophecy,' was published at the time in a book by Christopher Columbus.

Most scenes are described in their historically accurate locations. However, the tournament/meeting of Henry Tudor, Juana, and Phillipe Habsburg in 1500 took place near Calais (which was then English continental territory). I re-located the event to Windsor Castle, because Windsor is indeed the actual setting of a rendezvous between Henry Tudor and Juana, a few years hence.

# About the Author

SA Carney lives and writes in England and Spain. She was born in Panama, spent her early childhood in Turkey and attended high school in Seville, Spain.

She's a graduate of the University of Missouri-Columbia, with an M.A. from the University of Hawaii-East/West Centre.

She worked in Honolulu as a TV news reporter and documentary producer for ten years, before moving to London. She is married to Roger Wadsworth; their home is 14th Century hall house in Kent.

# More to Come

*Granada Gold* is the first of a planned Spanish/Tudor historical fiction trilogy.

If you would like more information about the sequel, please visit my website page,

www.sacarneyauthor.com

My website has up-to-date news, photos, book reviews, and links to relevant websites.

If you enjoyed reading *Granada Gold,* you can send online reviews to Matador, Amazon, and Goodreads.

Thank you!